# FASTROPE

---

## RACHEL HATCH
### BOOK 10

## L.T. RYAN

with

## FIONA RYAN

LIQUID MIND MEDIA

# THE RACHEL HATCH SERIES

# ONE

STRIKER SAT IN THE BACK OF THE FORD ECONOLINE PANEL VAN, STILL moving toward the destination. The roads became darker, murkier, as they moved through Panama City. He could only see a glimpse of his outer surroundings through the windshield, as there were no windows in the back.

About twenty minutes ago, they'd left their base of operations in the suburbs and now traversed through the seedier part of the city toward their target location. Flask drove, and their team leader, Cain rode shotgun. The lively banter of the earlier portion of their drive had quelled. The mental game required for such a task brought a hush upon the seasoned men.

Even though night had already fallen, the heat continued. Striker wiped at the sweat bubbling on his upper lip. The heavily tinted windows made it nearly impossible to see inside the front compartment, Flask and Cain remained maskless to reduce suspicion.

Flask's added subterfuge—disguise including a mechanic's gray coveralls and a hardhat—would provide the necessary cover once on site. A company logo was painted on the side of the van as well, at least to the untrained eye. When their task was complete, the magnetic decal would be removed, and the plates switched.

Colt and Woody sat on the opposite side of Striker. Unlike his silent demeanor, the two continued making quiet jokes between themselves. A stern glare from Cain brought their whispers to a halt.

Cain turned in his seat, and his attention now rested on Striker. The numerous missions and countless hours of training and preparation did little to minimize the power Cain wielded with just a look. "You're running point on this."

Striker nodded. The op plan had been ingrained into each operator's brain. Striker could run it with a blindfold on. Cain's reminder was part of the routine, a final safety check before they went weapons hot.

He turned to the rest of the group. "Boys, show's about to kick off. Game faces on. We're thirty seconds out from target." Cain's voice, gravelly and thick, carried a strong accent that harkened back to his Louisianian upbringing.

"Hard and fast," Colt said.

"Just like your last ten relationships," Flask said.

A burst of laughter erupted from the group.

"Lock it up," Cain boomed. "There'll be time for chewin' the fat when the day's work is done."

The chuckles turned into silence as each man began conducting a final inspection of his gear.

Striker did a press check on his Glock. Habits, good habits, were the hallmark of experience. He then slid the pistol into the Kydex drop-down holster strapped to his right leg. They'd swapped their camo uniforms for dark black fatigues.

"You look a bit pale, bud. Well, paler than normal," Swift, the smallest and quietest member of their team, said, throwing a friendly elbow in for good measure. "Everything good?"

"Right as rain," Striker said. Striker pulled on his balaclava, as did the rest of the team.

"I'll be tight on your ass."

"I wouldn't have it any other way." Striker's smile was veiled by the sweat-soaked mask.

"You lovebirds should get a room," Woody joked, cocking an eyebrow and following it up with a wink.

"Last turn comin' up." Cain held his balaclava on his lap. "We've got the skills and the firepower to overwhelm and contain our enemy. That doesn't mean lettin' your guard down."

"Roger that," the group acknowledged.

"Target is in sight. No tangos in view. Check your muzzle sweeps and watch your sixes." Cain's gaze was focused solely on the apartment building ahead. "Roll like thunder!"

"Strike like lightning!" The group gave their response in unison.

The van made a hard right turn, then slowed as they entered the complex. Flask pulled to a stop and cut the engine. The team remained motionless. Swift gripped the handle on the back door and awaited the command.

Flask stepped from the vehicle and donned his hardhat. His radio was connected to a wireless bone mic tucked neatly under the popped collar of his uniform.

"Mic check," Flask said as he walked from the vehicle over to the electrical box attached to the outside wall of the first-floor unit.

"Loud and clear. Proceed," Cain answered.

A few seconds later, Flask's voice transmitted over the team's radios. "Good to go."

"You heard the man." Cain slid the mask over his bald head. "Rock and roll."

Swift popped the back door. Within seconds of its opening, the team piled out. They moved in a tight line with their weapons drawn and held at the low ready.

Striker was on point. He crossed the concrete walkway and came to the outdoor stairwell leading to the second floor. Without hesitation, he ascended the cracked concrete steps toward the objective. He compensated for the weight of his gear, careful to tread quietly.

The team remained in tight formation. Striker felt Swift's body on his backside. Outside the door to the apartment, Striker waited and listened.

"I hear two voices," he said softly, allowing the bone mic to carry the message.

"Copy. Two tangos." Cain took up the rear, allowing him oversight of their operation. "Blackout in three—two—one."

On command, the power cut out and the light filtering through the bottom of the apartment's door went dark. Striker held his position as Colt stepped out from the stack carrying the sixty-pound ram at his waistline. The biggest man on their team had proven time and again his ability to force entry with unprecedented success. Colt pressed his right side along the hinge of the door. He hoisted the ram, lining it just above the knob and below the deadbolt.

Cain sent the greenlight up the stack with a squeeze of Woody's shoulder, who passed it onto Swift, who sent it to Striker. Upon receiving the silent message, Striker locked eyes with Colt and gave a nod of his head.

Colt twisted his hips, bringing the ram back. A moment later, he sent the steel cylinder forward. The door separated from the frame in a loud crack of splintering wood. The fractured door swung inward, the force of the blow nearly dislodging it from its hinges. Colt stepped back from the exposed entryway, tucking himself against the opposite side wall.

Swift stepped around Striker without exposing himself to the unknown threat inside. He tossed a flashbang into the darkness and peeled back. "Bang out!"

The team remained out of view, shielding themselves from the disorienting effects of the distraction device. A loud bang rang out from inside the apartment, accompanied by blinding light. The team had less than fifteen seconds to capitalize on the temporary impact.

As soon as darkness returned to the room, Striker stepped over the threshold, his weapon pressed out before him as he made entry. He took one step in, pivoted to the left, then moved along the wall. Swift, right on his heels, filled the void and moved in the opposite direction. Woody and Cain followed, flowing into the center of the small apartment's main space.

"Clear left. Clear right. Clear middle." Each member announced their status as they drew together into a loose v-formation facing the dark hallway ahead.

"Police. Search warrant!" Cain boomed. "Come out with your hands up."

A man emerged from the bathroom, pants dropped around his ankles. Even in the dark apartment, Striker could see a wild look in his eyes.

Cocaine a likely contributor. Striker recognized him from the mission briefing as their primary target, William Gladding, or Willie G as he was known on the street. A big-time dealer in the area with a penchant for violence.

"On the ground! Now!" Striker commanded.

Willie G stood still, mouth agape. His right hand hidden behind his back as he faced off in a stalemate with the darkly clad operatives who'd invaded his domain.

"Hands. Show 'em!" Woody yelled.

"I ain't goin' back! Ya hear me, cuz?" Willie slapped his head with his free hand. He started swaying and making a strange groaning sound that grew in intensity. "No way. No how."

"Don't do it, man." Striker tried to deescalate the situation.

"Kiss my ass, bitch!" Willie was nearly bouncing now. "Y'all wanna dance?"

"Show me your hands!" Woody's voice cracked.

"I got the shot. Give the word." Colt came up along Striker's right.

"Hold fire," Striker hissed.

The backdoor to the bedroom opened. A younger male, maybe sixteen, the spitting image of the deranged Willie G, stood in the backdrop. "Get the hell outta here!"

Willie turned. "Get back in that room and you don't come out for nuttin'. Ya hear?"

The boy hesitated. Willie's half turn had exposed the hand hidden behind his back and the long-barreled revolver dangling below his waist.

"Gun!" Woody called.

The alert caused Willie to spin. The gun, no longer hidden, hung down by his thigh. Striker saw a trace of hesitation in the drug dealer's eyes. He hoped the next tense seconds would allow for reason to sink in.

"Hold fire," Striker said just loud enough for his team to hear.

"Time's up. Put him down." Cain's words held no trace of emotion.

A deafening bang exploded in Striker's right ear. The muzzle flash lit up the dark interior. The impact of the round fired by Colt spun Willie's body into the wall.

The revolver was still clutched in his hand. Willie coughed up the blood filling his lungs. He screamed something inaudible before swinging the pistol upward. He shot wildly in their direction. Striker's team responded with shots of their own as they moved for cover.

A silence followed, broken by the agonal gasps of the dying man in the hallway. And then, nothing at all.

"Our time's up. We need to clear out ASAP," Cain said. "Striker on point. Moving to next threat."

"It's a kid," Striker protested. "What the hell are we doing?"

"This mission isn't complete."

"Moving to point," Colt said. He stepped into the hallway. The other members of the team took staggered positions behind him as they moved forward. Striker, now dislodged from his assignment, took up the rear.

Colt trained his muzzle on the blood-soaked man on the floor as he moved past. The two-man, Woody, stripped the gun and tossed it into the bathroom. He checked for a pulse and gave a non-verbal shake of his head, confirming what they already knew. Willie G was dead.

They reached the back room where the teenager had retreated. Colt gripped the doorknob and gave a slight turn. Locked. The poorly constructed apartment door would leave little in the way of a barrier for the large man.

"Tick tock," Cain said.

With that, Colt brought his knee up toward his chest and thrust his leg out. The bottom of his boot slammed into the door, breaching the bedroom.

The door shot inward. Bright flashes accompanied by the familiar sound of gunfire erupted from within. Colt spun and fell backward into Woody, who managed to break the fall. Cain aimed over Swift's shoulder and delivered three shots in rapid succession.

Striker watched as the third shot penetrated the front of the teenager's skull just above the bridge of his nose. The boy's stunned expression went slack as the brain began to shut down, his limbs giving out underneath him. Striker's stomach twisted into a knot at the sight. For a moment, he felt a disconnect from his surroundings.

Cain supervised with arms folded across his barrel chest. Woody, the team's medic, worked to stem the damage to Colt's shoulder by securing a pressure dressing. Swift moved to ransack the apartment, flipping cushions, opening drawers and cabinets.

Striker stood in the hallway, his gaze bouncing between the dead father and son. His mind reeled, the reward weighing heavily against the outcome. He felt Cain's stare bore into his back.

"Got it!" Swift called out from the bedroom closet. He exited with a large black duffle slung over his shoulder.

"Picked up chatter. Two minutes on the clock," Flask radioed.

The power to the apartment came back online, and the lights flickered to life. "Time to roll." Cain bumped Striker's shoulder as he moved past, the man's breath hovering in Striker's ear. "Get your shit together."

"Colt's stabilized. Ready to move." Woody hoisted the larger man up and positioned himself under the arm opposite the wound. Colt grunted as he was guided out of the apartment and down the stairs.

Striker was the last to leave, following behind Cain. Before rejoining the others, he looked back. Bags of cocaine were spread out across the kitchen table next to a scale.

He stepped onto the landing, his face and body slick with sweat. As he made his way down the steps to the first floor, he heard the creak of a door from above. His eyes shot upward, and he saw the apartment across the hall from their target location was cracked open.

Striker couldn't make out her features in this lighting, but he caught the pink and white pattern of the woman's pajamas. Her eyes widened as she looked across to the carnage, then shifted to rest on Striker. He held his index finger up to his covered lips. Panic replaced the shock he'd seen moments before, and she quickly backed away, reentering her apartment and shutting the door quietly.

Striker entered the van through the back door. The men inside were quiet except for Colt, who was stringing together a sequence of expletives as he held his hand against his bleeding shoulder. Colt's eyes settled on Striker, not hiding the rage held within them.

"That's not the way this is supposed to work." Striker took a seat beside Swift. The oversized duffle rested at the smaller man's feet. "That is not what I signed on for."

"We'll debrief later. Now's not the time." Cain didn't look back, his eyes transfixed on the road ahead as the van pulled out of the apartment complex.

Striker felt the knot in his stomach tighten. Sirens filled the heavy night air as they sped away.

# TWO

THE EARLY MORNING SUN SPRINKLED THROUGH THE TALL CANOPY OF TREES as her legs moved in rhythmic fashion, maintaining a steady pace. Hatch recalled the runs she'd gone on with her father before his death. Throughout their short-lived time together on this trail, her father had challenged, encouraged, and bonded with Hatch in ways that could never be replaced, nor forgotten. His words continued to echo in her mind and steady her hand in the most difficult of circumstances.

Hatch slowed to jog as she found herself by the brook that carved its way through the trail. She stopped near the large boulder nestled along the bank. Pressing her hands against the cool stone, Hatch stretched her hamstrings. The stone and the dirt around it were hallowed ground for her. It's the spot where, at age twelve, she'd found her father's body lying lifeless, surrounded and covered in the blood-soaked dirt. Over twenty years had passed since the day that had altered her life forever. Yet to Hatch, the memory of it was as fresh as the air around her.

Since that tragic day, life's experiences had added ample weight to the burdens she carried. The accumulation of which pressed down upon her like the boulder pressing against the earth beneath it. The most recent loss tore a hole in her heart she doubted would ever heal.

In the Oregon Pacific, Alden Cruise had placed his life before hers and the others stranded at the nuclear transplant facility out in the middle of the ocean. It's a debt she'd never be able to repay. Since his passing, she struggled to find meaning in her own life. Hatch tried to find solace in helping Graham Benson's widow get her footing after the devastating flood waters nearly destroyed her diner. It wasn't enough. And as much as it pained Hatch, being home with her family had alleviated some of the emptiness, but the void remained. Hard to move forward when the town held a constant reminder of the losses, old and new, she'd experienced.

Hatch stood back from the rock, her legs continuing to tingle from the exertion. She squatted low and moved her hips from side to side to stretch them. Then she touched her hands down to the soft earth around her feet. This gesture gave her a sense of connection to nature, like touching a light bulb and feeling the current passing through the filament.

In the quiet, she heard her father's words pass through her mind. *Darkness is a gift.* A much younger Hatch had been confused by the statement. Then her dad elaborated. *Darkness is a gift because it's only through it that we can truly appreciate the light.*

The words came with a gift of their own. The suffering she'd endured, if looked at with renewed perspective, could lighten her path going forward. She said a silent thank you to her father as she stood.

Hatch rubbed her hands together, releasing the dirt back to the ground. She took a deep breath before picking up her run and heading back toward home.

Her pace quickened as she made her way up the final leg of the trail that emptied out into the backyard of her childhood home. She sprinted the last thirty feet, pushing herself to feel the burn of Colorado's thin air sting her lungs. The rooftop came into view as she crested the hill, transitioning from the dirt path to the dew-covered grass surrounding the property.

The last time Hatch had been home, the house had been set aflame by the company she now worked for, nearly costing her family's lives. It was heavily damaged, but time heals all wounds. In the case of the house, time —plus Jed—had worked to heal the scars of that night.

Jed Russell had come into Hatch's life not too long ago. First, as a recluse who'd risked his life to save hers. Then, he'd found love in the form of Hatch's mother, Jasmine. Initially, Hatch had to get used to the reality of someone entering the vacant role left by her father's death. But watching him now on the scaffold above the backdoor, layering a fresh coat of paint to the side of the house, she was grateful.

"You're up early," Hatch called up.

"Looks like the kettle's callin' me black." Jed smiled, creases lining his leathery skin. "How's the trail this morning?"

"Same."

"Outrun any of those demons?"

"I keep trying but they keep a pretty good pace," Hatch said. He understood her in a way most of her family couldn't.

Jed had served as an infantryman in the Army. Actually, he and Hatch had cut their teeth in the same unit, the 101st Airborne Division's Screaming Eagles. Although their service had occurred at different times, they were both soldiers, and they both recognized it.

"Need any help up there?"

"Nah, I'm good. Just trying to get an extra coat on before breakfast. Your mother's up."

Hatch gave a two-fingered salute and made her way under the scaffold and into the house. The cool, dry morning air had already wicked most of the sweat from her body. The smell of her mother's famous brew outweighed any stench emanating from her body and pulled her into the kitchen.

"Morning." Hatch reached into the cabinet above the percolator to grab a mug.

"You never cease to amaze, my dear." Jasmine filled Hatch's cup.

"How so?"

"Always up before dawn. Pushing yourself even when you don't have to." Jasmine's eyes glistened. "Reminds me a lot of your father, is all."

"Then guess I'm doing something right." Hatch took a sip without adding anything to the bold blend.

"Let me add a dash of cinnamon. It brings out the flavor."

"As if it needed a boost." Hatch shot her mom a wink and extended her mug. After tapping a light layer of sweetness into her coffee, Hatch noticed a bit of hesitancy in her mother's expression. "Something on your mind?"

"Just worried about you."

"Why?" Hatch held the porcelain against her lower lip, savoring the aromatic steam flooding her nostrils before she took another sip.

"You've been through a lot. More than most could endure."

"I'm not the only one." Hatch didn't need to elaborate for the mother who'd lost both her husband and Hatch's twin sister to tragedy. "And there're people who've endured worse."

"True. But those people aren't my child. You are." The sheen of her eyes glossed over, and sadness permeated Jasmine's face. "I see the way you push away the pain."

"Pain is fuel, a driving force. I've accustomed myself to that." Hatch gave a half-cocked grin.

"Too much fuel can flood an engine."

"I'm good. Trust me." Although, Hatch wasn't sure which of them she was trying to convince.

"I know you're tough. You've proven that time and again. But that's not what I'm talking about." Jasmine put a hand on Hatch's shoulder, her fingers moving in gentle circles across the damp t-shirt sleeve. "It's your heart. Wounds like that, the invisible ones, take the most effort to heal."

Hatch knew what her mother was referring to. She'd dodged any mention of Cruise or Savage since coming home. Jasmine was right. The wounds were fresh. Invisible blood continued its trickle ever since she'd managed to lose both of the men she loved. Different circumstances had dissolved any chance of a future with either, each tragic in their own way.

"I just wish you'd talk about it. I wish you'd let me in." A solitary tear rolled down Jasmin's cheek. "I just want you to be happy, Rachel."

Hatch swiped her finger across her mother's cheek, snatching the tear from her face. "I know." She looked down into the steaming brown liquid of her coffee mug. "I'm just not so good at words when it comes to that kind of stuff. I'm a work in progress, I guess."

"Just know, I'm here if you ever need or want to talk. Jed too."

"I'm sure I'll get there someday."

"Just don't hold back too long. Emotions tucked deep have a way of crashing down like a tidal wave."

Hatch thought of the wave that had stolen a piece of her heart. Lifting her coffee to her lips, she downed the rest, allowing the burn in her throat to serve as a momentary distraction, the heat filling her chest.

"Will you be joining us for breakfast this morning?"

"I think I'm just going to jump in the shower."

"Well, when you're done, do you mind running on down to Harrigan's Market? I need a couple things for tonight's meal."

"Sure thing." Hatch conveyed a nonchalant tone, but she couldn't have felt further from it. Since returning to Hawk's Landing and learning that Savage had moved on, she'd gone out of her way to avoid any potential contact and had become a bit of a recluse, keeping to the house and the mountain trails surrounding it.

Jasmine handed Hatch the shopping list with a smile. The tearful look subsided, now replaced with a quizzical one. "I know things are different here now. But you're happy with it? I mean, you're okay with Jed and me?"

"He's a great man. A rare gem and I couldn't be happier for you both. I think it's been great for the kids, too."

"Never thought I'd be putting on the parenting hat again."

"I don't think you ever took it off." Hatch toyed with the list in her hand. "I don't say it enough. But I love you. I know I pushed you away, blamed you in some twisted way. And I was wrong to do so. I hope you'll forgive me."

"There's nothing to forgive." The waterworks returned. Jasmine pulled her daughter into a heartfelt embrace. "Our love is unconditional. Unbreakable."

Hatch felt her mother's thin frame tremble. She forced down the emotion, an involuntary protective barrier Hatch used throughout her life to harden herself to the pain.

"What's wrong?" A tiny voice squeaked from behind.

"Hey, there Daffodil." Hatch broke the embrace with her mother to muss the hair of her young niece. "Up early on a Sunday?"

"Couldn't sleep with the banging and clanging outside." Daphne's voice didn't hide the grogginess. She followed with an exaggerated yawn.

"Jed's trying to get this place ship-shape," Hatch said.

"I know, but why does he have to start so early?"

"Because that's how you get the worm, silly."

"Ew, yuck. Worms?"

"Speaking of worms, how'd you like some breakfast?" Jasmine had reset herself.

"Pancakes?"

"Pancakes it is."

"I'm going to get cleaned up and head out to the store." Hatch leaned down and kissed the top of Daphne's head. "And you, my little Daffodil, enjoy those flapjacks."

A big toothy grin stared back up at Hatch as she left the kitchen and headed for the stairs. She turned, meeting her mother's eyes. "Thanks."

"For what?"

"For loving me even when I'm unlovable."

Before her mother's tears could start again, Hatch disappeared up the wooden stairwell. She prepared herself for the trip into town. It struck her how much things had changed for her. Hatch had faced off against an unfathomable number of enemies in the past. Yet here she was, desperately afraid of confronting her past and the man she'd loved.

# THREE

Detective Maribel Santiago pulled up to her mother's quaint little house, a stark contrast to the clustered residences of Panama City just a few miles away. The sun was already burning brightly in the morning sky, and she could feel the sweat beading on her forehead as she opened the car door. Her daughter, Isabella, unbuckled herself from the backseat, eager to spend the day with Abuela.

"Come on, mija, we're running behind," Santiago called to Isabella, adjusting her police badge on her belt. Her day had not started well. A car accident on her usual route had caused a traffic jam, and now she was late for work. She could only hope that her captain would understand.

As Isabella bounded up the front steps, Santiago's mother, Rosa, appeared in the doorway, her hands on her hips and a frown etched into her face. "Mari, always in a rush," she chided. "You know this job is too much for you. You're always stressed, and it's not good for Isabella to see her mother like this."

Santiago sighed, a familiar tension building in her chest. This was a conversation they'd had countless times. She knew her mother worried about her, but she couldn't just give up her career as a detective. The job was dangerous, yes, but it was also fulfilling, and it allowed her to provide a good life for her daughter.

"Ma, we've talked about this," Santiago said, trying to keep her voice calm. "I can handle the stress. Besides, someone has to do it, right?"

Rosa pursed her lips, a silent reminder that she didn't agree with her daughter's choices. "You could find something else, something less dangerous," she insisted, her dark eyes filled with concern.

Santiago offered a tight-lipped smile, unwilling to engage in further argument. She could feel the seconds ticking away, and she needed to get to the station. "I'll be fine, Ma. I promise."

Santiago quickly bent down and wrapped her arms tightly around Isabella. "Be good for Abuela, okay?" she whispered into her daughter's ear, pressing a quick kiss to her forehead.

Isabella nodded, her brown eyes wide and solemn. "I will, Mami."

Santiago straightened, giving her mother a brief, apologetic look before dashing back to her car. As she climbed in, she could feel the weight of her mother's disapproval bearing down on her, but she had a job to do.

Her heart hammered against her chest as her silver Honda Civic screeched to a halt outside the precinct. The tires bit into the pavement, leaving behind black streaks that matched the urgency of her arrival. Santiago's eyes landed on the building, taking in the familiar brick facade.

As soon as the engine fell silent, Santiago bolted from the car, her boot heels striking against the concrete sidewalk with a staccato rhythm. She twisted her long, dark hair into a ponytail as she pulled open the front door to the main lobby. Warm air followed her in as she dashed inside, her breath coming in short, ragged gasps. The scent of stale coffee greeted her, followed by the pungent odor emanating from the two homeless men lingering outside the door to the public restroom.

Officer Jenkins, manning the front desk, glanced up from the reports he was reviewing. His tired eyes met hers, and he flashed her a casual greeting that never reached his eyes. "Mornin' Santiago."

Santiago's response was wordless, her exasperated look saying all that needed to be said. Her thoughts were a whirlwind of anxiety, leaving no time for pleasantries.

With the elevator's soft hum in the background, Santiago bypassed it in favor of the stairwell. The door slammed shut behind her, echoing off the stark, concrete walls. She attacked the stairs, hitting the steps two at a time.

When she stepped through the double doors of the bustling homicide department, the cacophony of urgent conversations, ringing phones, and the hum of police radio chatter assailed her senses. She hesitated, taken aback by the unusual flurry of activity. With a furrowed brow, she surveyed the room, noting the tense expressions on her colleagues' faces.

A major case must have come in overnight, one that had her fellow detectives on edge. Curiosity piqued, Santiago made her way through the bustling office. The low hum of activity amplified as she approached Captain Harold Parnell's office, his door wide open.

Before Santiago could knock, Parnell looked up from his desk and motioned for her to enter. His face was drawn, and there was a tiredness in his eyes that she hadn't seen before. " Come in. Shut the door."

She did as instructed, closing the door behind her and taking a seat across from the captain. "What's going on, Harry?"

Parnell sighed and rubbed his temples. "We got a messy one. A couple of drug dealers were gunned down in their apartment last night. The scene's a bloodbath. The brass is already breathing down our necks on this one."

"Who's working the case?"

"Malcolm," Parnell replied, giving a subtle roll of his eyes.

A bitter taste rose in Santiago's mouth at the mention of Derek Malcolm's name, the arrogant homicide detective who took every opportunity to undermine and belittle her. He was the type of cop who thought he was above everyone else, his smug smirk and condescending tone grating on Santiago's nerves like nails on a chalkboard.

"That guy couldn't find a clue if it was buried in his ass."

"Easy now. Don't need to go pissing in the wind." Parnell's eyes met hers, a flicker of sympathy crossing his features. "I know you two have your differences."

"That's an understatement."

"Listen, you're one of the best detectives we have. I know that, and so does everyone else."

"Almost everyone." Santiago shot a glance at Malcolm, standing by his cubicle and talking with one of the other detectives.

Their feud went back to their days in the academy where she'd bested him in nearly every aspect. The tradition had carried forward when the two hit the streets. Now, with both assigned to investigations, it would apparently continue without end.

"He's been assigned the case. His to work as he sees fit."

"You're telling me you don't see the link to the robberies I've been bustin' my ass on?"

"There's no proof this incident is related." Parnell threw up his hands and then ran them across the top of his thinning hairline. "Probably deal gone bad."

"Not buyin' it."

"Guess not. Doesn't matter either way. Last time I checked, you're assigned to the Robbery-Street Crime Unit. This is a murder case. Therefore, it belongs to Homicide."

"That's that then."

"I know you're not going to let this go. Just try not to step on too many toes. I don't need the brass pressing me any more than they already are."

"Got your eye on that chief hat, I see?" Santiago made little effort to hide the truth behind her sarcasm.

"Don't push it."

"Since when did solving crimes constitute *pushing it?*"

There was a courtesy knock at Parnell's door just before it opened. Santiago smelled the visitor and knew by the overwhelming scent of Old Spice just who was now standing behind her before turning to greet the chief.

"Mornin', sir." Santiago gave a tip of her invisible hat.

"Detective." The Chief stepped in, leaving the door open as an unspoken invitation for Santiago to leave.

"I'll keep you posted," Santiago said to Parnell before departing.

Santiago strode out of the captain's office and made a beeline for Malcolm's cubicle. He was hunched over his computer, focusing on an image from last night's scene. Santiago leaned against his cluttered desk, waiting for Malcolm to acknowledge her presence.

He didn't look up from his laptop, preferring to keep his focus on the screen. "This is a homicide, Santiago. Not a robbery," he drawled, his voice tinged with annoyance. "A bit lost, are we?"

"Not lost, just curious." Santiago's jaw tightened. She fought to maintain her composure, but the smug look on Malcolm's face tipped the scale. "Curious how long it's going to take your impressive investigative talents to connect the dots and realize this is the crew I've been hunting for the better part of six months?"

"Maybe if you'd done your job and made a case against these assholes, then I wouldn't be working a double murder."

Santiago felt the sting of truth in Malcolm's words. He was right, although she'd never let him know it. If she'd been able to snag the crew targeting the local dealers, it would've prevented this latest incident.

"Who's the vic?"

"Willie G and his son." Malcolm rubbed his hands against his face. "Shitheads killing shitheads. It's like a turd flushing a turd, and we're just the toilet paper cleaning the mess left behind."

"You're a true poet." Santiago craned her neck to get a better look at the image on Malcolm's computer. She saw the twisted body of Willie G. crumpled on the floor. She'd dealt with him several times over her career. He'd been no saint, but he also hadn't deserved such a gruesome death.

"Anything else I can help you with?"

"You said his son was also killed. How old?"

"Sixteen."

"Damn," Santiago muttered. Her mind flashed back to the last contact she'd had with Willie. It had to have been six years. She'd pinched him on an eight ball of coke. His son had been in the car at the time. She didn't remember much, except the boy had a brightness to his eyes. Santiago had hoped the child would escape the path set by his father and was saddened to see another life consumed by the street.

Malcolm sighed, finally looking up from his computer, his icy blue eyes meeting her unwavering gaze. "I don't need another pain in my ass. You got it?"

"If you've got ass pain, I'm pretty sure there's a cream for that."

Santiago heard a ripple of chuckles from the eavesdroppers manning the nearby cubicles. "As for the case, do your job and I won't have to be."

"If you don't mind, I have work to do." He waved his hand dismissively, as if shooing away a pesky fly.

Her lips pressed into a thin line, Santiago didn't respond, turning on her heel and marching back to her desk. She could feel the weight of Malcolm's gaze on her back, but she refused to let it get to her. As she reached her desk, she snatched up her notepad and pen, the urge to dig deeper burning inside her like an unquenchable fire.

"Where're you off to?" Detective Sanchez, one of the other members of her robbery squad, asked with a raised eyebrow.

Santiago's eyes flashed with determination. "To find some answers."

# FOUR

CAIN PULLED HIS TRUCK INTO THE DESOLATE LOT OF THE ABANDONED warehouse on the outskirts of Panama City. He cut the engine and stepped out of the vehicle. The air was thick with humidity, and the mid-afternoon sun beat down with an unrelenting fury threatening to incinerate every living thing in its path. Cain squinted and shielded his eyes with one hand, scanning the lot for any sign of his handler.

A figure emerged from the shadows of the crumbling building, a lanky man with wild, unkempt hair and a cigarette dangling from his lips. Gypsy ambled toward Cain with a fluid grace that belied his disheveled appearance.

"Thought you quit those cancer sticks," Cain said, his voice tinged with a hint of amusement.

Gypsy looked down at the unlit cigarette and smirked. "I'll be back to two packs a day if you can't keep your crew in line, Cain." His eyes snapped to Cain's face, the banter evaporating as the weight of the situation bore down on them.

Cain's smile faded, and he rubbed the back of his neck as he glanced away. "Yeah, about that..."

Gypsy stepped closer, the intensity in his eyes unwavering. "We don't have time for screw-ups, Cain. You know the stakes, and you know what happens if we fail."

Cain nodded, fully aware of the repercussions their actions could have. "I know, Gypsy. It's just..." He hesitated, struggling to find the right words.

Gypsy took a deep breath and removed the cigarette from his mouth. "Look, Cain, we all have our vices," he said, tossing the unlit cigarette to the ground and crushing it under his boot. "But we can't let them control us. Not now. This mission is too important."

Cain sighed, the responsibility of his role bearing down on him. "You're right. I'll make sure the team is ready."

"What the hell happened last night?" he asked, his voice taut with barely concealed anger. "Two men dead, Cain. Explain."

Cain leaned against a nearby wall, his arms crossed over his chest, and gave Gypsy a dismissive glance. "When you dance with the devil in a hot zone, you're bound to get singed. I'm just surprised we've made it this long without a little heat." His tone was casual, almost flippant, as if the deaths of two men were nothing more than a minor inconvenience.

Gypsy's face tightened, his eyes narrowing as he regarded Cain with a mix of annoyance and concern. "You know what's at stake here, don't you? We're not just talking about money. If we screw up again, there won't be anywhere left for us to hide. Our so-called friends won't be able to protect us."

Cain straightened up, his expression turning serious as he met Gypsy's gaze. "It won't happen again," he promised.

Gypsy scoffed, the sound sharp and dismissive. "Promises are just empty words, Cain. It's actions that'll pay the bills or fill the graves." He paused, his face softening slightly as he changed the subject. "How's Colt doing?"

A flicker of concern crossed Cain's face, but he quickly pushed it aside. "He'll live," he said with a shrug. "Bullet went clean through the shoulder. Woody patched him up, and we're putting him on light duty. We'll just say it's a weightlifting injury."

Gypsy nodded, his eyes never leaving Cain's face as he studied the other man for a moment. "Let's just hope that's the last of our troubles."

Cain's gaze flickered, his eyes clouded with apprehension. He hesitated before finally speaking up. "There's something I haven't told you."

"What?" Gypsy asked, his voice low and wary.

"We might have a problem," Cain replied, his jaw set.

Gypsy's eyes narrowed. "What kind of problem?"

Cain took a deep breath, swallowing hard. "There may have been a witness."

Fury swept over Gypsy like a torrential storm. His voice rose, unbridled, as he spat out his words. "And you're only telling me this now?" Rage simmered beneath the surface, threatening to erupt, but was quickly replaced with a sense of foreboding. "What about our exposure?"

"The neighbor across the hall," Cain said, "might have seen something."

Gypsy clenched his fists, his knuckles turning white. "Can this person identify any of you?"

"No," Cain assured him. "We were fully geared up, balaclavas and all. There's no way anyone'd be able to recognize us."

But Gypsy wasn't satisfied. He stared at Cain, his voice a low growl. "You better take care of this."

Cain met his gaze, understanding the unspoken directive to silence the witness. "I'll handle it."

Gypsy's eyes remained fixed on him, cold and unyielding. "Make sure there's no way the witness can ever talk again."

Cain nodded. As he turned to leave, Gypsy stopped him. "I'll keep an eye on things from my end," he said, his voice softer, but no less determined. "I'll let you know if any leads develop."

Gypsy leaned against the hood of his truck, his brow furrowed, eyes distant. Cain eyed him, seeing an edge of something left unspoken.

"Something on your mind?" Cain asked, his voice deep and steady.

Gypsy took a deep breath and met his gaze. "I've got a lead. A big one. The kind of score that might let us walk away for good."

Cain raised an eyebrow, intrigued. "What's holding you back?"

"Last night's mishap." The lines on Gypsy's face seemed to deepen as he frowned. "It's too hot out there right now. The risk of exposure is too damn high."

Cain cracked a smile and clapped his hand on Gypsy's shoulder. "When

God's work needs doing, Cain is able." His words were a well-worn mantra, a reminder of their shared conviction.

Gypsy looked away, his eyes taking on a far-off glint. "I'm still working on the logistics for our next op. I'll set a time to brief the team when everything's in place."

"We'll be ready to roll. Just give the word." Cain nodded and gave Gypsy's shoulder a reassuring squeeze.

The two men parted ways. Cain climbed into his Suburban and pulled away, the engine roaring beneath him. As he drove off, he glanced in the rearview mirror. Gypsy stood alone in the gathering dusk, a small flame igniting the tip of his cigarette, its glow reflecting off the lines of his face.

Cain couldn't help but feel the fine balance of their situation as he watched Gypsy fade into the backdrop. They were in deep. He'd been in worse and dug himself out. The playing field was different, but the rules remained the same. One directive trumped all others: When the gloves came off, survive.

# FIVE

THE SUN HUNG LOW IN THE SKY, PAINTING THE MOUNTAINOUS HORIZON with hues of gold and orange. Hatch gripped the steering wheel of her old truck, the rocky dirt road vibrating beneath her. Her eyes darted from the rearview mirror to the winding path ahead, the beauty of the landscape a constant distraction.

A sigh escaped her lips as she pulled into the small parking lot behind Harrigan's Market. It was a simple mom-and-pop grocery store, but its familiar charm offered her a sense of comfort, though she couldn't help but feel a little apprehensive. She felt her heartbeat quicken at the thought of running into Savage. Their last encounter plagued her, the memories of their past and the loss of what could have been still burned a hole in her heart.

The blame rested square on her shoulders. Since discovering Savage had moved on, she'd made every effort to shift the guilt, placing it on the time and distance between them. Deep down, she knew it was more. She knew it was her hesitancy to act on those feelings. Steady in battle, not so much in love. A soldier's curse.

As she moved through the narrow aisles, Hatch greeted people with polite nods and tight-lipped smiles. Her sister's death, over a year ago, remained a scar on the small town's history. The spitting image of her twin, Hatch always drew looks from the townsfolk who knew Olivia. To them, Hatch was a living ghost and a reminder of the tragedy.

Her fingers traced the edges of the canned goods as she continued down the aisles, trying to focus on filling the grocery list. Her thoughts wandered back to Savage. She tried not to picture his new life without her. It was salt in an open wound. But she comforted herself with the thought of his happiness, something long overdue and well deserved. She just wished she'd been the one to give it to him.

The weight of her own loneliness made her feel more exposed, more vulnerable than she'd ever felt in battle. She fought to steady her mind, on the verge of losing it in the middle of the small grocery store.

As she turned the corner, she caught sight of a tall, broad-shouldered man wearing a denim jacket. He was eyeing a stack of fresh corn. His back was to her, but she could see the dark hair sprinkled with touches of gray. Her heart skipped a beat and her face warmed.

Hatch felt a sense of panic and turned to extricate herself from the unintended encounter. As she spun, the hand cart she was holding collided with a precariously balanced tower of avocados. The dark green misshapen ovals spilled out onto the linoleum floor.

She considered dropping her belongings and making a mad dash for the door, but it was too late. The calamity drew the attention of the nearby shoppers, including the man she'd sought to avoid. Before she could make her escape, he turned.

Her mind did a backflip upon seeing the man's weathered face. It wasn't Savage. Relief washed over her, followed by disappointment.

The Savage doppelganger approached with a smile deepening the lines in his taut face. "Need a hand?"

"Thanks. I've got it." She bent to return the pyramid to its original height.

The man gave a nod and moved along. She watched him go and felt a balance return.

Hatch completed her shopping, grabbing the last item on the list. She bagged the fresh Brussels sprouts her mother had asked for, tucking them into the shopping basket alongside the other items.

The teenage cashier's eyes widened when she saw Hatch's scar, a twisted line that ran the entire length of her right arm, from wrist to shoulder. The wound she had earned while serving in the Army seemed to have a life of its own, pulling in the gazes of anyone nearby.

"I'm sorry," the girl stammered, realizing she'd been staring. She shook her head. "I didn't mean to."

Hatch shrugged it off. "It's okay. Took me a long while to get used to it myself."

The cashier began scanning Hatch's items and hesitated, curiosity etched on her features. "Does it still hurt?"

Hatch considered the question. "It did for a while." She didn't mention the memories that clung to the scar like smoke, the pain of that fateful day and the loved ones she'd lost burning as bright as the explosion that had nearly claimed her life. "Time has a way of mending the flesh and healing the memory."

As she paid for the groceries, the girl's expression shifted to one of admiration. "You must be really tough. I don't think I could handle anything like that."

Hatch offered a small, knowing smile. "Nobody knows how strong they are until it's time for them to find out."

With the transaction complete, she hefted the paper bags in her good arm and made her way out of the store, leaving the teenage cashier to contemplate Hatch's words.

Dust kicked up around her boots as Hatch strode toward her truck. The familiar sound of a vehicle approaching made her pause, her heart skipping a beat as a brown and tan SUV with the bright white letters Sheriff on the side rolled up and parked nearby. The pang of anxiety she'd felt inside the grocery returned, and Hatch couldn't help but feel a knot of unease in her stomach.

She watched as the door opened, and a familiar figure emerged. It wasn't Savage. Instead, it was the young, energetic Becky Sinclair, a deputy with the Hawk's Landing Sheriff's Office whom Hatch had worked with in the past. Relief washed over Hatch, a smile tugging at the corners of her mouth. Sinclair was someone she could trust.

Their relationship had been forged by the dangers they'd faced together. Hatch's experience and instincts guided Sinclair as they'd worked side by side. Hatch saw great potential in the young deputy and recognized the confident swagger Sinclair was starting to come into.

" Hatch!" Sinclair called out, her eyes sparkling with warmth. "I heard you were back in town. I was hoping you might swing by the station. Maybe even consider joining the department?"

Hatch shook her head, a wry smile playing on her lips. She appreciated the sentiment, but life had grown too complicated for that. Sinclair seemed to understand, her gaze softening as she looked at Hatch. They didn't need to talk about Savage or his new relationship. Some things were better left unsaid.

"How long are you planning to stick around this time?" Sinclair asked, curiosity tinting her voice.

Hatch shrugged, the uncertainty of her future weighing heavy on her shoulders. "I'm not sure," she admitted. "My path has a way of being dictated by forces beyond my control."

The two women shared a knowing look, each acknowledging the unpredictable nature of their lives.

"This place just isn't the same without you."

"Maybe that's a good thing."

"Not from where I stand." Sinclair's eyes swept her surroundings. "We always seem to be down a deputy. And with you, it'd be like hiring ten at once."

Hatch took the compliment in stride. "I'll keep that in mind. You take care of yourself. And watch your six."

"Always do. Learned from the best." Sinclair gave Hatch a wink.

With a firm handshake and a heartfelt wish for the other's well-being, they parted ways. Hatch climbed into her truck, her thoughts shifting to the road ahead. Life had a way of dealing unexpected hands, but it was in those moments where real character was forged. Sinclair was on that path. And whether or not Hatch admitted it to herself, she too was blazing a new trail in her life. Where it would take her was another story.

Right now, it was leading her back to her childhood home, to her family.

# SIX

IN THE OPPRESSIVE HUMIDITY OF PANAMA CITY, DETECTIVE SANTIAGO stood at the foot of a weathered concrete staircase, her brow beading with sweat as she assessed the scene of the previous night's grisly double homicide. The faint salty tang of the nearby gulf offered little reprieve from the suffocating heat as the breeze fought a losing battle against the relentless sun.

Santiago began the ascent. Her dark eyes were drawn to a trail of dried blood painting a macabre path along the stairs. The rusty hue of the remnants bore witness to the tragedy that had occurred.

As she neared the halfway mark, she spotted a boot tread embedded in one of splotches. Santiago squatted down to inspect the print further. She drew her cellphone from her pocket and began snapping photographs from various angles.

Santiago reached into her worn leather satchel and pulled out a paper ruler, laying it alongside the bloodstain. With clinical precision, she photographed the ruler and bloodstain together, ensuring the measurements were recorded. She jotted down several notations in her notebook.

As the sun continued to blaze overhead, she reached into her satchel again. Inside, Santiago found the blood evidence collection kit—a familiar friend in her endless pursuit of justice. She uncorked the water dropper contained in the kit and moistened the dried blood by adding several drops of the sterilized water. The once-hardened substance loosened, becoming pliable beneath her watchful gaze.

She uncapped the cotton swab and carefully retrieved a sample of the blood. Santiago returned the soiled swab to the evidence tube and closed it with a click. Santiago marked the evidence with the case number, the date and time of recovery etched with a steady hand, her initials like a promise upon the tape sealing the tube.

Her back cracked as she stood and straightened herself. The frayed ends of police tape hung from either end of the apartment door's frame, flapping in the light breeze.

Music sounded from the shabby unit. Santiago raised her hand to knock when the door opened to reveal a squat, rotund man, his jowls damp with sweat. Annoyance was etched across his face.

Santiago flashed her badge. "What are you doing here?" she asked, her voice low and steady.

"I'm the landlord," he huffed, wiping the perspiration from his brow. "Just trying to clean up this godforsaken mess." He waved a meaty hand toward the interior of the apartment, where the remnants of the investigation lay scattered like breadcrumbs. "Got to get this place ready for the next tenant, you know. Can't have it sitting empty."

The implication was clear: the man cared more for his pockets than for the tragedy that had occurred inside these walls. A slumlord through and through, Santiago thought, her lips pressed into a thin line.

"I'd like to take a look around," she said. The landlord's annoyance rippled like a heatwave, but he stepped aside, granting her access with a reluctant grunt.

"The detective in charge said I was free to do what I want, that the scene was cleared," he grumbled.

"I understand," Santiago replied, her voice betraying no emotion. "But I need to see for myself." She offered no further explanation, her eyes scanning the room with hawk-like intensity. His protests exhausted, the landlord lumbered out onto the landing and stood in disgruntled silence.

Santiago stood in the doorway, letting her eyes drink in the remnants of chaos before her. The bullet-riddled walls told the story of the violence that had unfolded. She stepped cautiously through the living room. Death had a distinct odor. The Florida heat added a unique note all its own. Even though the bodies had long since been removed, the lingering scent stung her nostrils.

A dark stain on the carpet along the hallway caught her eye, where Willie G had taken his last breath. The image from the file she'd reviewed earlier flashed in her mind. The bloodstain was diluted, the landlord's cleaning solution working its grim magic.

She made her way to the back bedroom, the scene of Willie G's son's murder. The landlord's efforts had not yet reached this room, the blood and brain matter staining the wall beside the bed. Santiago couldn't help but think of her own daughter, and the dreams they both harbored for a better life. Her daughter's father had abandoned them both, and the struggles they'd faced in his absence weighed square on her shoulders.

Forcing herself back into the present, Santiago took a deep breath and pushed those thoughts aside. She jotted down a few notes, but there was little left to glean from the already-processed scene.

"I'm all set," she told the landlord, her voice steady and professional. He nodded, stepping back into the apartment as she exited. The door closed behind him with a soft click, sealing the scene of tragedy.

Santiago eyed the apartment across the hall. She strode over and rapped her knuckles against the door with measured force. It wasn't long before the faint sound of shuffling echoed from the other side of the door.

"Who's there?" came a hesitant female voice.

Santiago cleared her throat. "Detective Santiago, Panama City PD," she replied, holding her badge to the peephole as a form of validation. She listened as the deadbolt slid back, followed by the jingling of a chain lock. The door creaked open. A Black woman greeted her, likely in her early thirties, eyes wide with a hint of nervousness.

Santiago re-pocketed her badge. "Mind if I ask you a couple of questions?"

"I already spoke to the officers last night."

"I'm doing a follow-up. Sometimes it helps to get a little space to let the mind settle." Santiago fished out her notepad. "Could I get your name?"

"Sophia White," she introduced herself, her voice wavering.

Santiago studied the woman's face, recognizing the flicker of hesitation in her eyes. She could tell something lurked beneath the surface, waiting to be revealed. Maybe it was just fear of the police or the repercussions for speaking with them.

"Were you home last night when the shooting took place across the hall?" Santiago probed.

Sophia hesitated, and Santiago could see the internal struggle playing out behind her eyes. "I didn't hear or see anything," she finally said, though her words lacked conviction.

Santiago knew she was lying, but she understood the woman's desire to keep her distance. In rough neighborhoods like this, the code of silence was a matter of survival.

Handing Sophia her business card with her cell number scrawled on the back, Santiago said, "If you think of anything that might help us solve this case, please call me. I promise anything you share will be kept confidential." She then shifted gears, inquiring about Sophia's family. "Do you have any children?"

"I have two," Sophia replied, her voice softer now and her eyes begging for this conversation to end.

Santiago seized the opportunity, using this maternal bond to appeal to Sophia's conscience. "Willie G may have sealed his fate with the life he chose, but his son didn't deserve to pay the price. He's lost his chance at a future, and even the smallest detail could make a difference in cases like this."

Sophia nodded, her eyes glistening with unshed tears. She closed the door, and Santiago heard the locks slide back into place before she made her way down the stairs and back to her car.

# SEVEN

STRIKER WALKED INTO THE MAKESHIFT TACTICAL OPERATIONS CENTER, THE smell of stale coffee and adrenaline hanging in the air. The room buzzed with the quiet chatter of his teammates–Woody, Swift, Colt, Flask, and Cain. They were assembled around the makeshift table, covered in maps and diagrams, all waiting for the last member to join them.

Striker caught Cain's steely gaze, a silent admonishment for his tardiness. He raised his eyebrows, shrugging his broad shoulders, and offered a weak apology. "Sorry, guys. Had to clear it with the wife first." The tension in the room eased, as a couple of the men smirked at the familiar excuse.

Cain, however, wasn't amused. He leaned forward, his graying hair and square jaw giving him an air of authority. "All right, let's get to it," he growled, cutting right to the heart of the matter. "We all know the op last night went smooth at the beginning. Prep and initial execution were flawless."

The team nodded, exchanging satisfied glances. But it wasn't long before the atmosphere in the room shifted, the weight of unspoken words hanging heavy in the air. Cain's gaze shifted to Striker. The others followed suit.

"But after we entered the apartment..." Cain trailed off, letting the sentence hang unfinished.

All eyes were on Striker now, and his face reddened with anger, the memory of the previous night's events fresh in his mind. He felt the heat of their stares, like daggers piercing his pride. He clenched his jaw and forced himself to meet Cain's gaze, his eyes a stormy mixture of defiance and regret.

It was clear they all knew where the mission had fallen apart, and Striker's role in it. He could sense their disappointment, their frustration. But this was a team—they lived and died together, sharing both victories, and failures.

Cain's voice cut through the tense silence, an attempt to reestablish order. "We'll debrief, we'll learn, and we'll move forward. Together."

Colt's eyes burned into Striker, his face a mixture of pain and anger. The bullet wound in his shoulder served as a reminder of what he perceived as Striker's hesitation to address the threat. The chaos that ensued had left them all on edge, and now the tension in the room hung thick like a fog, suffocating each one.

Striker had had enough. "This isn't some terror camp in Afghanistan," he fired back, frustration bubbling over, his words a mix of anger and desperation. "We're not a hunter killer squad."

Cain met Striker's glare with an unwavering stare of his own. "We don't make the rules of engagement. But we sure as hell follow them. When a threat presents, we address it with the force necessary to ensure mission success."

The others in the room voiced their support, their nods and grunts of agreement, acting as the jury delivering their verdict. Striker felt the tide of the room turn against him. "This was never the plan," he muttered, his voice low and hoarse. "I didn't sign up for this."

Cain's retort was sharp, unforgiving. "The minute you agreed, you knew the possibility of this kind of outcome."

Striker, feeling cornered and outnumbered, fell silent. Cain continued, his tone softening but still stern, "When the proverbial shit hits the fan, the only thing that matters are the men standing beside you."

Colt shifted in his seat, groaning as he clutched his shoulder. The pain was evident, his eyes narrowing as he cast a glare of judgment at Striker.

Cain's face took on a chilling seriousness as he locked eyes with

Striker. "So, my only question for you is, are you still standing with us?" His eyes narrowed, and the intensity of his gaze left no room for misinterpretation. "Because if not..."

The unspoken threat hung in the air, and Striker knew exactly what it meant. He swallowed hard, the bitter taste of defeat and resignation lingering on his tongue. He gave a slow, reluctant nod, knowing that his loyalty was no longer a matter of choice, but of necessity.

Cain's expression lightened like the first rays of morning sun breaking through a stormy sky as he addressed the motley group of hard men assembled before him. "I spoke to Gypsy earlier. He's gonna make sure this doesn't come back to bite us in the ass." He paused, letting his words sink in before continuing. "And that means we've got to do our part. We had a potential witness last night."

The news sent a ripple of agitation through the group like a stone thrown into a still pond.

Woody, a tall, lanky man with the demeanor of a coiled rattlesnake, asked, "What's the exposure?"

Cain shrugged. "Not sure. As of right now, that witness hasn't spoken to the cops. But if she changes her mind, then the problem becomes much larger. And we can't have that." This comment earned nods of agreement from all the men in the room, except for Striker.

Flask, the wiry and silent member of the crew, cleared his throat. "What's the play?"

Cain's gaze hardened like steel, his tone deadly serious. "There's only one option on the table."

The hidden meaning of his comment twisted a knot in Striker's stomach like a fist clenching around his insides. Cain's idea of *only one option* meant murder. And this time, it was an innocent woman's life on the line.

"The woman across the hall needs to go away," Cain said. "Permanently."

Swift, who had been hunched over his laptop, looked up. "I pulled up the information on her. Name's Sophia White. Looks like she's a single mother of two." The information about the woman Striker had locked eyes with on the previous night's raid sent a shiver down his spine.

"Should we draw straws?" Flask asked.

Colt, eyes ablaze and focused on Striker, said, "You were on point, and you dropped the ball." He glanced down at his arm in a sling and continued, "Don't think we need to draw straws. Striker should carry the responsibility."

Cain nodded his approval. "Looks like you're on deck."

Striker was left with only one acceptable response.

He steadied himself, feeling the weight of the decision like an anvil on his chest. He met Cain's gaze and said, "I'll handle it."

Cain's face broke into a predatory grin, and Striker knew there was no turning back.

Striker leaned against the wall, his muscular arms crossed over his chest as he listened to Cain's speech. The room was filled with the scent of stale cigarettes and sweat from the previous night's raid. Cain's voice was gravelly, his words punctuated by the rhythmic tapping of his fingers on the table.

"Rest up, but stay sharp," Cain said, the corners of his eyes creasing as he glanced at each member of the group. "Gypsy's already workin' on our next gig, and trust me, it's gonna be a game-changer." His gaze settled on Striker, and for a moment, the room seemed to grow quieter. "Hell, maybe it'll be enough to finally hang up your boots, Striker."

Laughter rippled through the room, but Striker felt the meaning of Cain's words slice at him like a knife. He'd been in this game too long, and retirement seemed like a distant dream, always just out of reach.

The group began to disperse, grabbing their gear and talking in hushed tones. In the back, a table sagged under the weight of the cash from the previous night's job.

Swift snapped his laptop shut and moved toward the table, his eyes darting between the money and the safe in the corner. Striker approached him, his heart pounding in his chest. "Hey, Swift," he said, his voice low and steady. "Can I grab my cut?"

Swift's eyes narrowed, suspicion gleaming in their depths.

Striker forced a smile and shrugged, trying to play it off. "The wife's got a couple home improvement projects lined up, and well, cash is running tight."

Swift hesitated for a moment, then handed Striker a thick stack of bills. Striker exhaled, the tension in his shoulders easing as he stuffed the cash into his duffle bag. He turned to leave, the door creaking open to reveal the humid Florida night.

"Striker," Cain called out, his voice cutting through the still air. "The witness needs to be dealt with tonight."

With a nod, Striker stepped outside, the door closing behind him. He climbed into his truck, the leather seat sticking to his skin. Pulling away from the safe house, he drove toward the heart of Panama City, the city lights reflecting off the dark water that surrounded it.

His fingers trembled as he reached for his phone, his heart pounding as he dialed the number he'd located earlier. The call connected, and he heard an older woman's gentle voice on the other end of the line.

# EIGHT

HATCH DROPPED THE GROCERIES WITH HER MOTHER AND TOOK THE TRUCK out to the lake. She sat on a fallen tree that served as a bench along the water's edge. The breeze flowing down the surrounding mountains cut across the water. The coolness pushed back the mid-afternoon sun against Hatch's skin.

Memories of her childhood summers spent splashing in the lake while her father worked to land a fish danced across her mind. The images shifted to a more recent one. The same lake became a watery grave for her twin sister. The taint of her death was in the clear blue in front of her. The lapping of rippling water carried with it a sadness.

Hatch looked down at her reflection, seeing her sister's innocence in the shifting surface. She spoke without words, apologizing for not being there for her, for failing to assume the role of mother her death had left behind. Hatch tossed a rock, shattering the stillness and scattering her reflection in the concentric circles extending out in all directions.

She stood and made the climb back to the truck. Putting the lake behind her, she headed home.

As she pulled to a stop on the dirt driveway, Hatch caught a glimpse of her nephew Jake on the grassy lawn, wielding a thin wooden staff. He spun the stick with precision and poise. He continued the precise movements of his kata as Hatch approached.

"Looking good," she said.

Jake stopped the staff, catching it against his ribcage and tucking it under his arm. He brought himself out of the low front stance he'd assumed when delivering his last blow to the invisible attacker and smiled. "Auntie Rachel! I just got moved up by my instructor to long-range weapons."

"I see that. I can tell you've been practicing. Your movements look sharp."

Jake beamed with pride. "I've also been learning knife defense. Wanna see?"

"Sure."

Jake set his staff on the ground and retrieved a wooden knife from the green belt wrapped around his waist. "Here. If you thrust it at my middle, I'll show you my move."

Hatch took the wooden replica from him. She brought it in line with her waist and smiled. "Ready whenever you are."

"Just don't go too fast. I'm still learning."

Hatch nodded and waited for the signal to attack. Jake stepped into a fighting stance, bringing both of his hands into a modified boxing position while keeping his fists open. He gave a slow nod and Hatch moved forward with the knife. Jake stepped to the side as the blade neared his midsection. His outstretched arm bent and he struck Hatch's forearm with his. The attack was deflected. The knife passed by Jake's body as he made a feigned punch to the side of Hatch's head.

"Nicely done," Hatch said.

"Not expert yet, but I'm getting better." Jake offered a sheepish grin.

"No doubt about it. Practice is the hallmark of any great fighter, and I think you've got the makings of one." Hatch handed the knife over to her nephew. "Want me to show you another defense?"

"Do I!" Jake swayed with anticipation.

"I just need your belt."

Jake looked confused, but quickly released the knot above his belly button and handed over the green belt. Hatch took it, then wrapped an end around each of her wrists leaving about a foot's gap between.

"Use the same attack."

Jake had a look of determination as he held the wooden blade at the ready. Hatch met his gaze and gave a nod of her head. Jake lunged forward. Hatch made a similar sidestep, but instead of using her arms to deflect the attack, she used the belt. After connecting with Jake's arm, she wrapped the belt around his forearm just above the wrist. In a swift motion, she twisted her body. The movement redirected the energy of Jake's thrust, throwing him off-balance and causing him to drop the knife.

Hatch caught her nephew before his momentary loss of balance landed him on the soft earth beneath their feet. She released him from the belt and gave him a pat on the head.

"Whoa. The guys in class are going to love it when I show them that move!"

"There's a lesson beyond the move."

"What do you mean?"

"Techniques are a great foundation. Without them, mastery is unattainable. But the real takeaway is that anything can become a weapon if the circumstances require it."

Jake nodded slowly, and Hatch could see the young boy processing the information. His hands toyed with the belt, wrapping it in the same way that Hatch had just demonstrated. She noted how quickly he learned.

"Can I try?"

"Sure thing."

Hatch and Jake spent the better part of the next hour drilling the new technique. As his skill with the belt improved, the speed and intensity at which the attack was delivered increased. They were both damp with sweat when they heard Hatch's mother call out to them from an open kitchen window.

"Why don't you two warriors give it a rest," Jasmine said with a smile. "Time for dinner,"

"One more?" Jake asked in a whisper.

"You heard the boss." Hatch mussed his hair. "There'll be plenty of time to practice. Let's get some grub."

Jake picked up his equipment and headed for the door. Hatch followed. The two entered through the back door and walked toward the kitchen.

Jasmine had her phone cradled against her cheek while she chopped an onion on the cutting board in front of her. "Hold on. Here she is now." Jasmine winked at Hatch. "It's for you."

Hatch wondered who'd be calling for her, especially on her mother's landline. She grabbed the phone, eyeing her mother as she turned to refocus on the prep work.

"Hello?"

"Is this Rachel Hatch?"

She couldn't place the man's voice on the other end. "It is. Who's this?"

"Jeff Ryker. I don't know if you remember me, but we spent some time together at the FOB a couple years back."

"Of course. Last I remember, you were six seconds behind me on the run time. Looking for a rematch?" Hatch noticed her mother eavesdropping, looking at her daughter and smiling. She stepped out of the kitchen and into the hallway, the cord stopping her from going any farther.

"Seems like forever ago."

"Tell me about it." Hatch noticed a seriousness to his tone and dropped the banter. "Everything okay?"

"It's complicated." Ryker paused. The sound of a helicopter filled the air.

"You calling from overseas?"

"No. I'm stateside now. Based out of Panama City."

"Nice change from the sandpit."

"Guess so, yeah." His words had an edge to them.

"What's up? I mean, you must've gone through some trouble to get this number."

"I called around. It's listed as your home of record contact." Ryker grumbled something inaudible before continuing. "Not sure why I called. Probably shouldn't have bothered after hearing you're no longer in. Just thought maybe you could help me out."

"If I can, I will. Shoot."

"I'm kind of mixed up in something. Not sure where to turn. I know you were in criminal investigations, figured you might be able to—I don't know—point me in the right direction."

"Tell me what's going on and I'll see what I can do."

"Not sure where to start. Probably shouldn't even involve you. Just didn't know where to turn. You were always a straight shooter."

"I try to be. Let me ask you something. Why me? Why not reach out to someone local?"

"That's the complicated part. I'm in a bit of a jam." Ryker's voice flickered in and out.

"Ryker, you there? It's pretty choppy on my end."

A brief silence, followed by a low crackle of static, before words began to filter in. "Shit service. I'll call you back a little la—"

The line went dead. Hatch walked the phone back to the kitchen and stuck it back on the receiver. Her mother had a knowing smile etched on her face.

"Who's the gentleman caller?" Jasmine raised a playful eyebrow.

Hatch fought a childish eyeroll. "An old friend."

"From your military days?"

Hatch nodded. Her mind was still processing both the surprise of the call and the cryptic information Ryker had doled out.

"Everything okay?" Jasmine now mirrored the seriousness of Hatch's expression.

"Not sure. We got cut off."

"If it's important, I'm sure he'll call back." Jasmine scooped the onions from the cutting board into the pan on the stove. "In the meantime, why don't you go get freshened up so you can join me in getting this feast in order?"

"Will do." Hatch stepped out of the kitchen and headed upstairs. The conversation replayed in her head. What stuck out wasn't so much the words, but the desperation in the stalwart soldier's voice.

# NINE

SOPHIA WHITE STOOD IN FRONT OF THE ELECTRIC STOVE, WATCHING THE pasta boil. The once stale shells rumbled around inside of the bubbling, steaming liquid. Her two young boys had set the dinner table and were sitting down, laughing together and waiting for her return with the macaroni and cheese.

Sophia watched the resilience in her children's playful banter. After the previous night's tragedy, most kids would have been traumatized. Not her boys. Sure, they'd been scared. But when they woke this morning, the new day brought a cleansing to the events of the preceding night. Although it showed their strength of character, it also worried her. The environment where they were forced to live was hardening them in a way she'd hoped to avoid.

They'd been on their way to a better life when things took an unexpected turn. Her husband had fallen victim to drugs and alcohol after losing his job. That was bad enough, but at least he was home. On the good days, they'd been a family. All that went down the drain like the hot water she poured from the pot to the colander in the kitchen sink.

Drunk behind the wheel, a crash resulted in the death of a young man. That, compounded with her husband's history of abuse, had landed him a sentence of ten years for involuntary manslaughter. In doing so, he'd condemned Sophia and her kids to a prison of their own.

Sophia gathered some shredded cheese and milk from the fridge, pouring it onto the pasta, along with some seasoning. Stirring it around with a wooden spoon, she lifted a small bite out of the bowl and took a nibble. Gooey and savory, well worth every penny.

The boys always loved it when she made macaroni and cheese. She'd perfected the recipe years ago and had made it at least once a week since. In light of recent events, Sophia deemed it the perfect comfort meal to settle both the stomach and the mind.

"Mama." Her oldest looked up at her with his bright brown eyes and curly hair framing his face. "Can we visit Dad soon?"

"I'll have to check my schedule." Sophia paused at seeing the disappointment in her son's eyes. "Maybe I can get off early one day next week. Does that sound like a plan?"

The sadness dissipated, but not completely. Prison was an ugly place. Sophia worried about them seeing their father in that way, the damage it would cause. But she also weighed it against the value of maintaining the connection with their father.

Her husband had gotten clean while inside. Sophia now saw the man she'd fallen in love with. He was nearing the end of his sentence, and she held out hope his newfound sobriety would extend beyond the walls of the prison. But hope was something she kept on a high shelf and rarely reached for.

Sophia set the steaming bowls of pasta in front of her children. Just as she stepped off to grab the milk to refill their glasses, a knock sounded at the door. Her heart skipped a beat, but seeing the nervous glances between her children, she composed herself.

The boys held their forks but made no move for the mac and cheese before them. Fear had frozen them in place, dashed their carefree spirits from just seconds ago. The dread of the unknown returned in full measure. Sophia held a finger up to her lips. They nodded in unison.

The knock was now louder, followed by a man's voice. "Miss Sophia, I need to speak with you."

Sophia noticed the voice was not forceful or threatening, but it was commanding. She looked down at her feet. One pointed to the door, the other down the hall to the small bedroom the three shared. Her body was just as confused as her mind.

She took a deep breath and steadied her nerves. Fear was getting the best of her, Sophia told herself. She started moving towards the door. Sophia pretended not to notice the look of panic in her boys' eyes or the fact her youngest had reached out with his hand in an effort to stop her.

Sophia stood in front of the door. Her eyes scanned the locks. Even though she knew they were set, as was the routine anytime they were home, Sophia's unease had forced her to check twice. Satisfied, she leaned forward. Her face hovered half an inch from the door as she squinted through the peephole.

"Can I help you?" she asked, mustering as much confidence as she could find.

"I just need a quick word," the man said. "Won't take but a minute."

"If you're with the police, I already spoke to them earlier. Spoke with 'em twice."

"What needs to be said can't be done through closed doors."

"Sure it can." Sophia scanned the apartment until she put eyes on her cellphone. It was on the table in the living room, eight feet from where she stood. "I'll call the cops if you don't leave this instant."

A long, slow groan rolled out from the man. Sophia watched him intently. He didn't look like a killer. Sophia grew up in some of the roughest areas of Florida and had seen a killer or two in her day. She didn't see it in the man patiently waiting on the opposite side of the door for her.

She committed the mystery man to her memory, should she need to identify him to the police later. A white male with a medium build wearing an untucked button-down shirt and a pair of jeans. He looked like a casual version of the detective she'd spoken to the other night. The man outside her door carried a small black duffle bag slung over his shoulder.

Her hand touched the metal of the doorknob, and she heard her youngest gasp. The sound gave her pause.

"Miss. Sophia. Whether or not you open this door might very well decide whether you and your children live."

His words temporarily paralyzed her with the effectiveness of a taser. Sophia turned to her two boys who stared at her. She then pointed down the hall. Her oldest shook his head, a defiant look came over him. Since their father had been locked away, her twelve-year-old had recently begun to try to fill his shoes as "man of the house." Sophia gave an uncharacteristically stern look and pointed down the hall with more agitation in the gesture.

Both boys quietly got up from their seats, lifting their chairs and being careful not to scrape the linoleum floor. They abandoned their bowls of mac and cheese as they tiptoed down the hall. Sophia saw the worry on their faces as they closed the door to the bedroom, their eyes etched with fear before the door closed completely.

Sophia exhaled the breath she didn't realize she'd been holding and unlocked the door. She half-prepared herself for the man on the other side to burst through the moment after. But no act of sudden violence befell her and, after pausing only a moment longer, Sophia opened the door.

"Mind if I come in?"

"Don't see much of a choice in the matter." Sophia stepped aside.

The man entered. Sophia closed the door behind him as he surveyed the room.

"My kids aren't here. They're with their father for the night."

The man looked past Sophia to the three steaming bowls of pasta set out on the small kitchen table. "You don't have to fear me. I'm not here to harm you."

"Then what're you here for?" Her nerves gave way to anger. "You're not a cop. Then who are you? And why is it so important to the wellbeing of my family that you speak to me?"

The man didn't answer. Instead, he unzipped the duffle hanging from his shoulder and reached his hand inside. Sophia's heartbeat doubled, and she threw her hands in front of her face in an involuntary defense against whatever threat was coming her way.

"Relax. I already told you, I won't hurt you."

His hand withdrew from the bag. It was no longer empty. In it was a wad of cash, the likes of which she'd never seen before. She waved her hand. "Wherever that came from, you need to take it back. Don't want anything to do with it."

"Take it. Don't argue." He handed the money over to her.

Sophia wanted to push the brick of cash back into the visitor's hand, knowing wherever this money came from had to be illegal. Feeling it in her palm, a seemingly invisible magnet stopped her ability to release it. "I don't understand. This is about last night, isn't it? Some type of hush money."

"Not exactly."

"I told the cops nothing. I don't want trouble. I know how things work." She looked from the cash in her hand to the man standing in front of her. "Tell whoever you work for that I don't need to be bought. I have no plans of talking."

"You don't understand what's at play here." His voice lowered. "Your vow of silence won't matter. Not in this circumstance."

"Then what's the money for?"

"Your survival." He let an exasperated sigh. "These people will stop at nothing to remove any risk of exposure. Right now, that's you."

"And they sent you here to pay me off?"

"They sent me here to kill you."

The flatness in his tone conveyed the truth behind his words. Sophia swallowed hard. "Then why are you bringing me this instead?" She fumbled with the cash.

"Because I can't. I won't." His head shook as if he were arguing with another voice inside his mind. "What matters is that you take this cash and get away from this place as quickly as you can."

"Where can I go?" Sophia looked around her squalid apartment.

"Nowhere they can track you." He pointed at the money. "There's ten thousand there."

Sophia's jaw dropped, but no words came out. Ten thousand? That's more money than she made in six months working two jobs. She felt a wave of dizziness come over her.

"I know it's not enough to keep you tucked away forever, but hopefully it'll carry you through until I can get things cleared up, make it safe for you and your kids to return."

Sophia nodded, her mind flooded. "I'll figure something out."

"Whatever you do, it needs to be now. Tonight. As soon as I leave, the clock will be ticking."

"Tonight? How will I get—"

"This isn't up for debate." The man cut her off. "You want to live, your kids to live, then you pack what you can carry and get the hell out of here." His voice grew louder, and he took a brief pause to return to a more level tone before continuing. "Cash only from here on out. Harder to trace. Don't call anyone, friends or family. No one can know where you're going."

"How will I know when it's safe?"

"Not sure." He wiped a bead of sweat from his forehead. "Wish I could say more. I'm sorry for all of this."

Sophia saw a sadness sweep over the man's eyes. In that moment, something clicked. Something she recognized about the man but couldn't place until now. "It was you."

"Huh?"

"Last night. It was you on the stairs. The one who looked up at me."

"I didn't mean for any of this to happen."

"Won't you be in trouble? Won't this come back on you?" She held the green brick up. "Why is my life more important than yours?"

"Innocents always trump the guilty." He cast his eyes downward. "I have to reap the consequences of my actions, I can accept that. But I'll be damned if I'm going to allow good people to fall because of my mistakes."

"You seem like a good man."

"Maybe I was once. Not sure that still holds true."

"Why not go to the cops? They have ways of protecting people, right?"

"There's no protection the police would be able to provide. Not for you. And definitely not for me. The best you can hope for is to stay off the radar long enough for me to figure out how to make this right."

"How can I repay you?"

"Stay alive." He made a half attempt at a smile before turning for the door.

As the mystery man stepped back onto the landing, Sophia called to him, "'The good shepherd lays down his life for the sheep.' It's a bible verse that's always brought me comfort, knowing good people were out there protecting us. I hope there's someone out there looking after you."

"Me too. God knows I'll need someone." He moved quickly down the stairs and out of sight.

Sophia closed the door, resetting both locks before rushing to the bedroom. She knocked and entered. Her eldest held a baseball bat at the ready. His younger brother tucked behind him. Seeing his mom, the bat fell to the floor, and he rushed into her arms. She scooped both in a tight embrace.

"Pack a bag. Not toys. Just clothes, toothbrush, that kind of stuff."

"Why? Where are we going?" Her youngest asked.

"We've got to move fast." She saw the look of panic wash over her children. She did her best to hide her own. "I'll explain when we're on the road. But for now, just do as I ask, please."

The boys nodded and set to the task, offering no further protest. Sophia went into the closet, pulled out an old suitcase, set it on the floor, and began tossing in clothes and essentials.

She didn't know the man who'd just been there. But the conviction in his eyes and the seriousness in the words he'd spoken were enough to make her a believer. He said the clock was ticking. As she loaded their belongings into the bag, Sophia heard the unmistakable ticking of each passing second, and she dared not waste a single one.

# TEN

THE CLOCK ON THE WALL READ TEN MINUTES PAST EIGHT, ITS TICKING A
soft but constant reminder that Santiago was still at the station, buried in
paperwork instead of being home with her family. The guilt gnawed at
her, and she couldn't shake the feeling that she was failing them. She
picked up the phone and dialed her mother's number, hoping to smooth
over the rough edges of the day.

"Hey, Ma," Santiago said, her voice a mix of exhaustion and apology.
"Sorry I didn't call earlier."

Rosa's voice was thick with reproach. "You know, Mari, every time you
miss a meal, a little piece of Isabella's heart breaks. Your job is tearing this
family apart."

Santiago clenched her jaw and shut her eyes as though tensing them
would deflect the sting of her mother's words. "I know. It's just this case.
It's a big one."

"But what about your daughter?" Rosa insisted. "When are you going to
make her your priority?"

The question hung in the air, heavy and unwelcome. Santiago forced
herself to stay calm. "What about being able to provide for my daughter?
This job is how I do that, doesn't that count for something?"

Rosa sighed, her voice softening, but no less disapproving. "Tonight, I made empanadas. Isabella was so excited. We waited as long as we could. I've put the leftovers in the fridge. They'll be there whenever you get home."

The image of her daughter waiting expectantly by the window, a plate of still-warm empanadas on the table, was too much. Santiago's heart sank. "Can I talk to her?" she asked, her voice barely audible.

Rosa sighed and called for Isabella, who picked up the phone a moment later. "Hi, Mama," she said, her voice a sweet, innocent balm to Santiago's aching heart.

"Hey, sweetie. I'm so sorry I missed dinner," Santiago said, her voice cracking with the weight of her guilt. "I promise I'll be home in time to tuck you in and read you a bedtime story, okay?"

"Okay, Mama. I love you," Isabella replied, showing no trace of the guilt her mother had just levied against her.

"I love you too, sweetheart. See you soon." Santiago hung up the phone, staring at the pile of paperwork on her desk, each sheet a barrier between her and her daughter. She knew, deep down, that her promise might be another one of many broken, and that knowledge tore at her.

But for now, all Detective Maribel Santiago could do was take a deep breath, push aside the guilt, and dive back into the case.

Santiago pushed her chair back, her muscles tense. She needed answers, and she knew just where to find them. She stalked over to the only other person still in the office this late. Detective Malcolm leaned back in his seat, his hands behind his head as though he were sprawled out on a lawn chair enjoying a summer's day.

At the sight of Santiago, Malcolm slumped forward and hunched over his keyboard, eyes narrowed in concentration that had been nonexistent just moments ago.

Santiago leaned against the cubicle's retaining wall and stared down at the man who pretended to ignore her. "Didn't mean to interrupt your naptime," she said, her voice dripping with sarcasm.

"When you play in the big leagues, you need a seventh inning stretch. Don't worry, this tank's got plenty of gas."

"If you're done referring to yourself as both an athlete and car, let me know, and we can discuss police work."

His initial answer came in the form of an eyeroll followed by a sigh of resignation. "What is it that you feel the need to bother me about now?"

"Did you bother to take any blood samples from the apartment stairwell last night?"

Malcolm paused and slowly looked up from his computer, annoyance etched on his face. He flipped through the notes on his desk until he found the evidence log. He scanned it with the intensity of an accountant reviewing a tax return. It was all for show, because Santiago could see from where she stood that there was no record of it.

"No," he finally replied.

"Why not?"

"Not that it's any of your business, seeing as how you're not assigned to the case," Malcolm said, "but it was assumed to be transferred from the first units on scene."

"Whose assumption?"

"Mine."

"Well, you know what they say about assumptions," Santiago snorted, shaking her head. "I'd say you assumed wrong."

Malcolm's eyebrows shot up, and he leaned back in his chair, his own anger flaring. "And how, pray tell, did you come to that conclusion?"

"Because I was there. I walked the scene."

"You had no business being there," Malcolm snapped back. "This isn't your case to work, Santiago. You don't get to meddle in my investigation. Just like I don't go messing with yours. It's what's referred to as professional courtesy."

"Professional and courtesy are two words I've never associated with you." Santiago leaned in closer. "And you, Malcolm, have no business working a crime scene period if you're not willing or able to consider all potential evidence. It's sloppy, and it's beneath the standards of this department. So which is it? Sloppy or lazy?"

Malcolm's face flushed red, and he opened his mouth to retort, but Santiago had already turned on her heel and stalked away, her point made. She could feel Malcolm seething in his seat, the air thick with resentment. Santiago had no doubt she'd struck a nerve.

Santiago looked at her watch, then over to the evidence collection kit sticking out of her satchel. She considered the advice of Captain Parnell about playing nice with others. The thought was fleeting. Malcolm's reaction to her comment about the stairwell led her to believe her theory would likely be cast aside and with it the blood sample she'd acquired. When met with an obstacle, two options were available. Let it block the path. Or find a way around. Santiago didn't let things stand in her way, and, in her world, she was left with only one.

She made the decision to deliver the sample herself. The lab was closed at this time of night, so that would have to wait until tomorrow. She looked at the supplemental reports she'd downloaded from the server and printed, skimming them again. She knew both officers, not well, but well enough.

Santiago picked up her phone and called the main desk officer on duty. A gruff voice came responded, "McCluskey."

"It's Santiago. Just wanted to check the roster to see who's on duty tonight."

"Lookin' for anyone in particular, or did you want me to read the list?"

"Baxter and Green. I just need to follow-up with them from last night's shooting."

"Thought Malcolm was runnin' the show on that one."

Santiago rolled her eyes, knowing Malcolm likely made it known that any and all inquiries into the case were to be fielded through him. He'd done it before. It didn't surprise her now. "I'm helping out on this one."

"Gotcha." McCluskey hummed to himself. "All right. Looks like Baxter's off tonight. Green's on duty. Pulled an extra shift. Give me a sec and I'll see if I can get a hold of him."

"Thanks." Santiago tapped her fingers on the edge of her desk as she waited.

"Green's tied up at the moment. Working a three-car pile-up. Not sure when he'll be clear, but you can try to reach him on the radio, if you need to."

She eyed her watch again, this time thinking of the promise she'd made to her daughter. "It's no biggie. I'm heading out. I'll hit those guys up tomorrow. They're back on regular, right?"

"Yup. Workin' second shift, so you can probably catch them right after roll call."

"Sounds like a plan." Santiago hung up the phone.

All her potential leads would have to wait until tomorrow. The job had given her the gift of time, and she planned to use it wisely. She closed the satchel and left her cubicle. Santiago passed Malcolm's desk, neither offering a comment. The day had come to an end, and each had hung up their gloves, leaving the verbal sparring match for another time.

She made quick work of getting to her car, then sped away. Her thoughts of justice turned down to a low hum. Her mind was focused on more important things, like her daughter.

# ELEVEN

Hatch came down the stairs, the aroma of the meal calling to her. The hum of her family's voices filled the air. Hatch's mind was still too preoccupied by the conversation she'd had with Ryker to fully tune into the noise below. She pushed back the myriad of questions stacking in her brain as she reached the first floor. She told herself to let it go for the time being and be in the moment, not dwelling on the past or the unseen future. Not an easy task for Hatch.

The kitchen hummed with an inviting warmth, permeated by the mouthwatering scent of garlic butter chicken sizzling on the stove, tendrils of steam dancing upwards beyond the reach of the overhead vent. Jasmine stood at the center of it all, enveloped in an apron adorned with a vibrant array of poppies, her skilled hands sautéing the succulent meat, butter, garlic, earthy mushrooms, and a touch of white wine. She moved with the practiced ease of someone deeply familiar with the culinary arts.

Off to one side, Hatch took on the role of sous chef, a small hand towel casually thrown over her shoulder. Her eyes narrowed in concentration as she masterfully wielded a knife, deftly halving Brussels sprouts before tossing them into a waiting bowl. The kitchen seemed to dance around them, alive with the shared rhythms of their culinary choreography.

Hatch's eyes drifted from her task, seeking out her mother. She found

Jasmine's gaze already locked on Jed, whose eyes were equally transfixed by Jasmine. The pair exchanged a warm, secret smile, lost in their connection before returning to their respective duties, cheeks flushed and smiles lingering, reminiscent of giddy schoolchildren with a newfound crush. The sight warmed the very depths of Hatch's heart.

She remembered the years when Jasmine's once-sparkling eyes had dimmed, robbed of their light by her father's death. It was a darkness that had persisted through Hatch's enlistment in the military, and even after her return in the wake of her sister's untimely passing. It seemed as if nothing could rekindle the fire that had once burned so brightly in Jasmine's eyes.

And yet, when Jed Russel entered their lives, the light returned, as though awakened by some long-forgotten enchantment. The joy that had lain dormant for so long was rekindled, and Hatch knew it was more than just the flicker of an ephemeral flame. That light was here to stay, a testament to the enduring power of love and connection.

Jake and Daphne moved gracefully around the dining room, their excitement palpable as they set the table. "Why don't you both take a seat and relax a bit? Have some water," suggested Jasmine, her voice warm and soothing.

The two children shared a knowing glance, their giggles bubbling up as they filled their glasses with water and claimed their designated spots at the table. Their eyes wandered to Hatch, the air heavy with expectation. Sensing their gaze, Hatch looked up and locked eyes with the pair. With a mischievous grin, she crossed her eyes and stuck out her tongue, the impish act igniting peals of laughter from Jake and Daphne. Hatch's own laughter mingled with theirs.

Returning her attention to the task at hand, Hatch expertly tossed the Brussels sprouts, ensuring each one was coated with olive oil, salt, and pepper. Her mother scooped the seasoned sprouts into a separate frying pan, the sizzle of their cooking filling the kitchen with the bold aroma. The heat was high, ensuring a perfect crisp.

As the meat absorbed the rich flavors of the wine butter glaze and the Brussels sprouts roasted in the pan, Hatch and her mother assembled a vibrant salad, their movements in sync. Over the past few weeks, they had evolved into a formidable team in the kitchen, a newfound bond strengthening with each meal they prepared together.

"Still bothering you, I see." Jasmine spoke without looking up from her task.

"Not sure what you mean."

"You can't hide from me." Jasmine set the knife down on the cutting board in front of her. "You may have hardened your exterior over the years since you've been away. But I can still see through it. Past your invisible coat of arms and into your heart." Jasmine pointed a soft finger to Hatch's chest, between her collarbones.

Hatch let a low groan escape. She followed it with a roll of her eyes.

"Don't dismiss the power of a mother's love." Jasmine put a gentle hand on Hatch's shoulder and looked deep into her eyes. "I was able to do the same to your father."

Hatch felt like a child again, her mind reverting to memories of a time before tragedy had stolen that time of life from her. "I know. I remember." It had been a long time since Hatch allowed the memories to resurface. She'd buried them deep during the years of anger and frustration. The time she'd spent upon this latest return had worked to unearth them.

"He was a stubborn ass. Just like you." Jasmine smiled. Her eyes watering along the edges. "And just like him, you can't help but put the lives of others above your own."

"That was his code," Hatch said, avoiding her mother's gaze. "I just follow it."

"I know. I just wish more for you. I fear you'll follow him to an early grave."

"Death comes for us all. I've accepted that. I just choose to face the reaper head on." Hatch gave her mom a wink and peck on the cheek.

"What was that for?" Jasmine asked, taken aback by the uncharacteristic show of emotion by her daughter.

"Count it as a drop in the bucket for the love I've held back for too long. I'm going to have to write you an *I owe you* for the rest."

"I'll hold you to it." Jasmine wiped at her eyes with the sleeve of her shirt. "Darn onions always get to me." She cleared her throat. "Now, is everything okay? That call seemed to throw you off a bit."

"Just a blast from the past. Caught me off-guard is all. I'm sure it's nothing." Hatch busied herself by drizzling a tangy vinaigrette over the crisp bed of greens.

"I've seen that look before. I've also witnessed the aftermath. Just do me one favor."

"What's that?"

"Promise me never to forget who *you* are. Staying centered is what keeps us balanced. It's the anchor that keeps us from being swept out to sea. Find that, and you'll always be able to bring yourself ashore."

"Promise." Hatch followed by giving her mother a playful nudge with her hip. "Since when did you become so prophetic?"

"I've always been this way. You're now just starting to hear it."

"What are you too gossiping about over here?" Jed chuckled, sneaking behind Hatch's mother and pulling her into a loving embrace.

Jasmine rolled her eyes, a playful smile dancing on her lips as she broke free of the hug and carried the large salad bowl to the table.

A warm, content silence enveloped the gathered family, the room buzzing with anticipation for the meal ahead. Jake and Daphne broke the silence with a fit of giggles, their laughter infectious as it spread throughout the room, causing everyone else to chuckle.

As the laughter subsided, Jed cleared his throat. "How about I say a blessing?" His voice resonated with sincerity, embodying the love and gratitude that filled the room.

The family joined hands around the sturdy oak table, their fingers intertwined as if forming an unbreakable chain. Religion had never been a cornerstone in Hatch's life, something she'd battled with in the face of tragedy. But in the weeks of home-cooked meals and the routine of the nightly blessing preceding each one, she'd reached her peace with the idea of a higher power, although the jury was still out on how this played into her life and the path she'd walked.

Hatch felt her mother's warm, reassuring hand on her left, and Daphne's small, soft palm on her right. The innocent touch of the young girl sent a ripple of tingling sensations through Hatch's hand and forearm, stirring a feeling she'd long forgotten. A smile formed on her lips, softening the harsh lines that had become her trademark.

"Dear Lord," Jed began, his voice resonating with sincerity and warmth. "We come before you with grateful hearts to thank you for the bounty of delicious food and the exceptional company. We're truly blessed to be gathered here as a family, united in love and safety. As we venture forth on the paths you've laid out for us, we pray that you'll watch over us, guide us through the challenges we face and ultimately reunite us as a family, unscathed. May the battles and wars fought in our daily plight forge our understanding of the bigger purpose we all serve."

Hatch opened her eyes to see Jed staring at her. The others kept their heads down, awaiting the closing word. "And for those of us who shepherd the flock, may our staff be strong and our will stronger. Let the meal we consume fuel us for the road ahead, and unforeseen challenges lying in wait." He gave her a knowing wink. "Amen."

The rest of the family repeated his last word in a low whisper and released their hands. The energy surging through their connection slowly dissipated. It was a subtle reminder to Hatch that although life's journey was fraught with danger and uncertainty, the bond of family was a beacon of hope and strength. Or, as her mother more aptly put it, the anchor that tethers.

The clatter of cutlery filled the room as everyone dug into their meal, exchanging pleasantries about the events of their day, the fickle spring weather, and the week that lay before them. Hatch listened but offered little to the discussions taking place. Her mind drifted back to the phone call.

The silence between bites of dinner weighed painfully as Hatch paused to take a sip of water, letting it glide down her throat and clear away the tension. "I've made up my mind," Hatch began, her voice steady despite her unease. "I'm heading to Florida to check on an old friend."

"No. Not again," Daphne said. Her eyes watered as she set her fork on the plate.

"It's not what you think. I won't be gone long."

"You've said that before." Her arms now folded and her lips drawn down in a pout.

"I know. And I know I haven't always been able to follow through." Hatch looked to Jed. His understanding eyes brought her comfort. "Sometimes life has a way of forcing our hand. I wish it wasn't true, but like the wind and rain, we don't always have control."

"Then promise you'll come back."

"I'll promise you, I'll be back as soon as I'm able." Hatch could see from the unchanged expression on her young niece's face, the words didn't reassure her.

"Not good enough. I want you to promise you'll be back. Soon."

"Your aunt is called to these things. It's like your love of art," Jed said. "When you see a piece of paper, what's the first thing you do?"

Daphne remained stalwart in her defiance, as Jed waited for the answer.

"C'mon now. What do you do?" He gently pressed the issue.

"I grab my markers."

"You sure do." His weathered features drew up into a smile. "And you make your masterpieces with those markers, don't you?"

Daphne's cheeks reddened. Her arms released and the tension of moments ago fell away. "I guess so."

"No guessing. I know. I've seen your work and I can attest to it." He pointed the sprout stuck to the end of his fork in Hatch's direction. "And your aunt's just like you in that way. Not in her ability to draw, but in her ability to help people."

"That's right," Jasmine added in her support.

"Her canvass is different. She sees people in need the same way you see a blank page. Her skills come from a different place, learned over many years in some of the harshest conditions imaginable."

"I guess it makes sense." Daphne looked at Hatch with sad eyes. "It's just that I hate when she leaves."

"Me too, my little daffodil." Hatch gave her niece a peck on the head.

"When do you leave?" she asked. Her words squeaking out past the emotion she held back.

"Tomorrow morning. Maybe it'll turn out to be nothing but my over-active imagination, and I'll be back before you know it."

Daphne made no further protest. She picked up her fork again and began poking at the food in front of her.

"Well, let's not turn Rachel's last meal with us into a sad one," Jed said. "Let's enjoy each other without a thought about what tomorrow will bring and count our blessings we have today to share as family." His words jump-started the energy of earlier, and the conversation resumed its joyful hum.

Jake leaned across the table in Hatch's direction. "I'll keep practicing while you're away."

"I know you will." She gave her nephew a smile. "You keep it up, and you'll be teaching me a thing or two before you know it."

The meal continued until all the plates were empty. Each did their part in the clean up by bringing dishes to the kitchen sink. Jed assumed his role as dishwasher.

As the room cleared, Jasmine took Daphne up to draw her a bath. Jed caught Hatch's elbow before leaving. "I'm well aware I ain't your father, and I could never hope to fill those shoes. But I need you to know that you'll always have a place here, and I couldn't be prouder of the incredible woman you've become."

"Thank you, Jed. I don't think I've seen Mom this happy since... well, since Dad. We're all grateful to have you in our lives. And it seems you've been a remarkable father figure for Daphne and Jake."

Jed smiled, humility etching his face. "Guess it's time for you to get ready for your next adventure."

"Guess so." Hatch pondered the thought.

"Do me a favor."

"What's that?"

"Try not to get in over your head." Jed was solemn now. "I know your code. I know the cost of its burden. Just watch your six and come back here in one piece."

"Is that an order?"

"Yes ma'am."

Hatch gave an impromptu salute. She then leaned in and landed a kiss on his cheek.

Hatch turned and made her way upstairs. Her mother left the bathroom, nearly colliding with Hatch. She saw the unease in her mother's expression. Words were not needed to convey the thoughts and emotions running through each other's minds. They locked in a quiet hug. Hatch took in the serenity of her mother's embrace.

The unknown of tomorrow was pushed into the recesses as she took in the moment, collecting this memory of her mother's warmth as a keepsake for the journey ahead.

# TWELVE

THE SUN WAS A FAINT EMBER ON THE HORIZON, CASTING ITS LAST GLOW over the barren landscape as Cain barreled his Suburban down the back-road. He looked at his watch. The team would already be assembled. Rank had its privileges, including being fashionably late. Although he tried not to abuse the position, his preoccupation with getting things back on track was paramount, and the meeting he'd just had with Gypsy was vital to ensure the future opportunity and the payout now within their grasp.

The vibration of his cell phone in the center console's cupholder broke the hypnotic hum of the engine. He fumbled with it, the light illuminating his face with an eerie blue glow. Gypsy's name flashed across the screen, and Cain pressed the answer button and set it on speaker.

"Miss me already?"

"A situation's come up." The other man's voice was terse, the tension in his tone conveying the seriousness of his call.

Cain dropped the friendly banter. "Go with it."

"Just got some disturbing info about our witness."

"She talking?" Cain's mind swirled with the possibilities of such an outcome. Everything they'd worked for was now on the line. The results, if she were able to identify them, or at the very least, point the cops in the right direction, could have disastrous ramifications for all involved.

"No."

"What's the problem, then?"

"She's gone."

Cain breathed a sigh of relief. "Told you I'd have my guys take care of it."

"And therein lies the issue." Now Cain was thoroughly confused. He hated it when he had to pry out information. His life revolved around brevity. Gypsy had a flair for the dramatic, something Cain despised about the man but had developed a tolerance to. This evening was testing the boundaries of his patience, and Cain felt his blood begin to boil.

"Reached out to the landlord. Doing my due diligence, ensuring this thing's contained." Gypsy's words trailed out with the smoke from his cigarette that he blew into the receiver. "She's ghosted."

"Ghosted how?"

"I mean packed up and gone," Gypsy said, his voice tense with urgency.

"Maybe it was made to look that way. Don't jump the gun on this. Give me a second, and I'll touch base with Striker and see what's up."

"I don't think you're understanding me."

"Then help me get there. Because right now, I'm hard pressed to believe a problem even exists."

"She didn't disappear in the way you and I expected she would. Not in the way which would ensure her never having the ability to speak to anyone, ever."

"Not sure I like where you're going with this."

"You don't have to like it. You just have to accept it." Gypsy followed with a raspy cough. "The landlord saw her leave last night."

"You're saying he tipped her off? How far can she get? I can't imagine a woman without means is going to have many options when it comes to relocating."

"I guess that's the million-dollar question. This might help answer it. The landlord said he saw a man he'd never seen before leaving the area not long before Sophia made her hasty departure."

"Could've been a coincidence," Cain muttered, not wanting to accept the implications this new information presented.

"No such thing. Not in our line of work," Gypsy said. "Plus, this guy's got no reason to lie to me. He puts money above people every day of the week, and he was paid good money for the intel on Willie. He's also well-aware of what I'd do to him if he did."

"Doesn't make sense." Cain's orders were followed. That simple. It'd been that way since he could remember, regardless of the tasking.

"Well, it better start making sense, and fast. Who'd you send to handle it?"

"Striker." Cain slowed the Suburban and pulled to the right side of the road. Cain grunted and slammed his fist on the dashboard, the final piece fitting into place. "He took his share of last night's haul before leaving to take care of the issue."

"And that didn't throw up a red flag? We've always agreed that there should be no financial purchases outside the norm following an op. We established that cool off time for a reason."

"I don't need the lecture. I also know that each one of us have dipped our hand in the till from time to time." Cain's voice projected over the rumble of the truck's engine. Rage filled his eyes, angry at himself for not seeing it before now. "He told Swift he had some big expenses coming by way of his wife's honey-do list."

"Hindsight is twenty-twenty, my friend. Once you've got it, you can't look at things the same way."

"Striker's never failed me before."

"That's not a completely accurate statement, now is it? Not based on what you told me about last night's op." Gypsy let out a slow exhale and continued before Cain could offer an answer to the contrary. "He's getting cold feet on all this. You said so yourself."

"He's a good soldier. One of my best men."

"He's on the fringe. And you know it."

Cain didn't answer. He absorbed the vibrations of the engine rumbling through his body, mixing with the surge of adrenaline coursing through his veins.

"Sounds like someone didn't follow your order. Maybe you didn't make it clear enough. Either way, it's a two-headed problem now. And both need to be cut off."

"You know what you're saying? What you're asking of me?" Cain's knuckles were snowcapped mountains clutching the steering wheel.

"The toughest taskings fall on the broadest shoulders. And this one's resting square on yours."

"He's a good man. A husband and father."

"We're all good men. We all have families. It's about the greater good."

"Poor choice of words." Cain released his grip and wiped the sweat from his palms on his fatigues. "There's got to be another option."

"I don't see one. Trust me, I ran the gambit before making this call." The stroke of the lighter indicated the chain smoking continued. "His foot's already pointing toward the door. How long until that sense of righteousness comes back to bite us in the ass? How long until he decides enough is enough and points authorities in our direction?"

"He wouldn't."

"Are you willing to bet your livelihood on that?"

Cain met the question with silence. He knew the truth of the matter. If this was anyone else, he wouldn't have put up this much resistance. As a tactician, he understood what needed to be done. As a friend he'd faced hell together with, he was downright conflicted.

"Your lack of response is answer enough for me."

"I'll handle it." Cain's words travelled through clenched jaws.

"Got a plan on how this is to go down?"

Cain looked ahead to his destination. The gated arm descended after a vehicle passed through. "One just came to me. One that will at least honor the life he lived prior to all of this."

"Once this situation is under control, we can proceed with the other op. Time is of the essence if we plan to take advantage of this new opportunity."

"I understand. I told you I'd handle it."

"I trust that you will."

"What about the witness? She's still a threat." Cain preferred to shift the focus to someone other than Striker.

"I'm working on it from my end. As soon as I locate her whereabouts, we'll resolve that issue and make sure she never tells her side of the story."

"Do we even know if she's got anything worth telling? I mean how much could she have seen anyway?" Cain made a last-ditch effort to salvage the spiraling situation. If he could downplay the witness, maybe he could spare Striker the repercussion. Doubtful, but worth a shot, at least for his conscience's sake.

"No way to know. If Striker had done his job, he could've extracted that information beforehand." Gypsy's voice crackled like static on an old radio.

"True."

"I don't like this anymore than you do. It kills me to be the one making this call."

"It kills me to be the one taking the next step." Cain let the truth of his feeling toward the matter at hand bubble over into the tone of his voice. A man noted for his toughness, he suddenly felt the walls of that façade crumbling around him.

"The ends will justify."

"They better."

"It's settled then."

"I'll handle it tonight," Cain said, staring out into the darkening sky. "But you'll have to bat cleanup on this one when it's all said and done."

"I'll do what needs doing. Count on that," Gypsy said. "And for what it's worth, I'm sorry it had to come to this."

"You and me both."

"I guess you've been forced to live up to your callsign, Cain."

"I am my brother's keeper."

"Sometimes salvation requires sacrifice."

"You'll know when it's done. Just be prepared to hold up your end. This next op you've got planned better make all of this worth it." Cain tapped his finger on the screen, ending the call without waiting for a response.

Cain remained unmoving as he sat a quarter mile from the place where he'd have to do the unthinkable. This drive usually filled his heart with a sense of belonging, a connectedness to something greater than himself. It had been that way for nearly a quarter century. But not now. After tonight, he wondered if he ever would again. He did something out of character and reached into his glove box. He pulled out the metal flask, uncapped it, and brought it to his lips. The burn of whiskey did little to settle his unease.

The hollowness inside his thick chest spread throughout his body. He replayed the history he and Striker shared in a highlight reel running across his mind. The world was different then. The one he inhabited now shook the foundation of everything he held true. One thing was certain. After tonight, there was no going back.

# THIRTEEN

FOUR ROWS OF MEN WERE SEATED ON THE WARM CONCRETE OF THE TARMAC. The sun had set, and the slowly rising moon bathed the water beyond in its pale glow. The breeze was light but refreshing against the relentless humidity blanketing them as Ryker took in the Marines before him. The helicopter they'd be using for tonight's training was being run through its preflight ritual checklist.

Ryker looked at the other members of his training cadre standing nearby. Sergeants Roger Kastner and Mark Li stood off to his right. Staff Sergeant James Woodrow on his left. The four hardened, battle-tested Marines stood at parade rest. The trainees remained silent as the instructor cadre waited for the arrival of First Sergeant Calvin Hurley.

Headlights swept over the group as an SUV rolled to a stop by the hanger bay. A door slammed, and the silhouette marched forward. Even in his shadowed form, Hurley was an intimidating sight to behold. The First Sergeant eyed the Marines on the ground as he passed. The intensity of his gaze was enough to sober a man out of a drunken stupor. Tonight, that look in his eye was amplified.

"Marines, the task you will perform this evening is a culmination of the last two weeks of training you've endured. Stepping off those skids is a rite of passage. What you learn here tonight will serve you well on the field of battle. It will give the advantage of speed and surprise as you descend upon your enemy." Hurley's voice rumbled like distant thunder.

"Oorah!" erupted from the seated Marines.

"There's no better way to bring a devil dog into the fight than this beautiful bitch behind me." Hurley gave a half-turn and pointed toward the helicopter. "This is the Marine UH-1Y, better known as Venom. She's as mean and nasty as they come. Mounted with two fast rope gantries for rapid insertion. In this Marine's opinion, there's no finer way to crash the party."

Another round of Oorahs reverberated across the tarmac.

"To demonstrate the requisite skills needed, there's no better group of Marines than the cadre standing before you." Hurley ran his eyes over each member of his team and came to rest on Ryker. "With that said, I turn this evening's briefing to Gunnery Sergeant Jeff Ryker, one of the best Marines I've ever had the pleasure of serving alongside. Gunny, take it away."

Ryker stepped forward from the line of instructors. He paced slowly in front of the men seated in front of him. The eagerness in the eyes staring up at him reminded Ryker of a younger version of himself, the man before the man. It brought him back to a simpler time, one free of the heavy burden accumulated on the battlefield. These Marines had yet to face those tests. Some would fail, some would die, and others would become legends. Time and experience would answer the question. Right now, it was Ryker's job to give them one of the skillsets they'd be using along that journey into the hell that is war.

"This is it, Marines. This is your opportunity to test the limits. Some of you think you're ready for tonight's task."

"Oorah, Gunny!" they boomed back.

"Others of you are secretly holding your breath in hopes that bird back there has a malfunction and cancels the mission." Ryker cocked an eyebrow.

This drew a ripple of chuckles from the group before a "Lock it up, Marines!" exploded from Sergeant Kastner.

A hush fell over the group. Ryker continued. "Make no mistake. Fear is a part of battle. Those who deny it are missing the opportunity it provides. It sharpens the mind like the fine edge of your K-Bar."

Ryker stepped out to the edge of the formation. He looked over at the helicopter as the pilot and copilot sat in the cockpit. "You're going to be one hundred feet off the ground when those ropes drop. Doesn't seem like much, but trust me, a fall from that height is a death sentence."

No Oorahs this time. Some of the excitement had shifted to the nervousness at facing the cold, hard reality of the task ahead.

"I see the thought I've planted in your heads is starting to take hold. Good. Let it. Let the thumping of your heart and the adrenaline coursing through your body be fuel. Consume it, control it, and harness its true power." Ryker caught Hurley watching him more intently. A sudden wave of worry bore down on him, causing a brief pause in his speech.

Ryker cleared his throat and turned his back on his First Sergeant, squaring his body to the trainees' attentive eyes. "The Venom has the capability of housing ten Marines. That's ten hard-chargin', ass-kickin' leathernecks capable of exiting the bird in under a minute. Lot of damage ten Marines can bring to the fight."

"Oorah!" The energy of their response ramped back up.

"Staff Sergeant Brunson is out injured this evening, so there'll be four of us running the demo."

"Five," Hurley said. "I'll be making the drop as well. Only way to lead is from the front. Ain't that right, Marines?"

"Oorah, First Sergeant!" The group responded in unison.

"Once we're up, you won't be able to hear the commands. Remember your training and when it's your turn on deck, one of the cadre members will be in the bird with you to guide you through." Ryker looked at the team assembled. "These men will keep you safe. Listen to them, and you'll be out the door and down the rope. Simple enough?"

"Oorah, Gunny!"

"Oorah, Marines." Ryker turned to face the cadre. "Ready to rock n' roll?"

The group smiled back. Woodrow cocked an eyebrow. "Thought you'd never ask."

Hurley made eye contact with the flight crew. He twirled his finger in the air, and a moment later the whir of the engine swelled and the rotors began slowly spinning, increasing their speed with each rotation. The five men broke into a slow jog, dipping their heads as they moved under the blades and in through the side doors of the chopper. Kastner and Li went to the opposite side of Ryker and Woodrow. Hurley was the last onboard, entering behind Ryker and taking a seat with his back to the pilot compartment. Ryker and Woodrow faced out the door they'd entered. The trainees would be required to strap into their seats. But this was old hat for Ryker and his fellow instructors, and they opted for simply gripping the harness, holding on as the bird began to lift off the ground.

Ryker held his strap, gripping tight with his gloved hand as the helicopter hovered above the Naval Air Station, the place he'd called home for the better part of the last year. The city was a constellation of lights. The moon shined bright to the east, casting a line of white across the black water that lay just beyond the edge of the base.

Hurley leaned in close, his knee brushing against Ryker's thigh. "You take care of that thing?"

Ryker smelled the faint odor of whiskey on his First Sergeant's breath. He'd known Hurley and the man's love of drink, but had never smelled it before an op, training or otherwise. The smell of it now was disconcerting.

"I did what needed to be done," Ryker said with as much confidence as he could muster.

"I know." Hurley spoke just loud enough to be heard above the noise of the cabin.

It wasn't so much the words his First Sergeant said, but more the way in which he said them that sent a ripple of concern down Ryker's spine. Coupled with the look in Hurley's eyes, Ryker was unnerved. He looked to his left, but Woodrow seemed not to hear, his eyes looking out the open door awaiting the command of execution.

The co-pilot twisted in his seat. "Good to go!" He shouted loud enough to be heard over the roar.

"Drop rope!" Hurley commanded.

Ryker stood, keeping hold of the strap while he kicked the thick, braided rope piled on the floor of the cabin. The metal arm of the gantry swung outward, and the rope unraveled, disappearing over the skid to the ground below.

He released his grip on the seat's harness, exchanging it for the rope as Ryker moved closer to the edge. Hurley stood and watched as Sergeant Li did the same before edging closer to Ryker.

"Roll like thunder!" Hurley boomed.

"Strike like lightning," the group responded. Ryker only mouthed the words, his effort doused by Hurley's last comment to him.

"Step out!" Hurley commanded.

Ryker shifted his body, turning his back to the water. He gripped the rope with both hands as he reached out with his right leg. He felt the whoosh of wind generated from the spinning blades above as he sought purchase with the middle of his boot on the skid below.

Just as he reached the metal plank, Hurley's body collided with his. The unexpected impact sent Ryker spinning away from the cabin. He fought for control, but failed to maintain his footing on the skid. His hands slipped free of the rope. The deafening roar of the helicopter's interior evaporated.

Ryker felt the rush of air as he fell backward. The rapid descent silencing the world around him. The next few seconds were distorted by the racing of his mind. He locked eyes with Hurley for a split second as his First Sergeant leaned out from the cabin, holding onto the rope intended for Ryker. Hurley's eyes offered a silent apology, one that Ryker did not accept.

He thought of the decisions leading to this moment as the tarmac below waited to receive him. His only solace was in the hope that his sacrifice had saved another from a similar fate. It was a question he'd never know the answer to.

His body struck the hard concrete. His final thoughts were of his wife and child as the whirling blades of the helicopter above faded into oblivion.

# FOURTEEN

THE SHARP SCENT OF JET FUEL PERMEATED THE AIR AS HATCH STEPPED OFF the small aircraft, her boots thudding on the sunbaked tarmac. Florida's relentless sun bore down, its rays a far cry from the crisp, cool air of her childhood home nestled in the mountains and forests. Already, she could feel the sweat threatening to spill from every pore in her body, reminding her of the sweltering heat she had left behind years ago.

Hatch hefted her worn duffle bag over her shoulder, her muscles flexing beneath her tanned skin. She fished out her smartphone from the pocket of her cargo pants, her fingers navigating the touch screen to find Ryker's name. She'd saved his number yesterday when he'd given her that cryptic phone call. With a single press, she initiated a call back.

The phone rang once before cutting off, the robotic voice of the voice-mail system greeting her instead. A furrow creased Hatch's brow as she disconnected and dialed again, hoping for a different outcome. The call went straight to voicemail as Hatch pushed her way through the airport doors, the sign for ground transportation beckoning her onward.

Deciding it might be better to text Ryker, Hatch typed out a brief message: *I'm in town. Thought I'd stop by. Address?* She slipped her phone back into her pocket as she entered the airport, grateful for the twenty-degree temperature drop. The air conditioning was a welcome relief.

Hatch made her way through the bustling crowds, following the signs and the flow of people towards the ground transportation and rental cars. Her progress was aided by escalators and moving walkways that seemed to stretch on for miles. Some stood idly on these devices, content to let the machines do all the work, the sight of which made Hatch want to roll her eyes. She elected to work with the machinery, not rely on it entirely.

Ignoring the strange glances from other passengers, Hatch strode purposefully up the escalators and along the moving walkways, determined to reach her destination faster. Thankfully, people moved aside as she approached, clearing the path for her relentless advance.

Finally, Hatch found herself in a dimly lit parking garage, the air thick with the smell of exhaust fumes. Before making her way to the car rental stand, Hatch checked her phone once more. Ryker still hadn't responded. Instead of trying again, she dialed another number.

"Tracy, it's Hatch. I was hoping you could help me with something."

"Hello to you too," Jordan Tracy said with a hint of amusement, his voice barely audible above the cacophony of voices and white noise in the background. "Straight to the point, I see." A senior member of the private contractor firm Talon Executive Services, Tracy had access to information Hatch could only dream of seeing for herself. Plus, it helped that she was on his good side.

"Pleasantries are wasted air." Hatch glanced around, ensuring she was out of earshot of anyone nearby.

Tracy chuckled. "All right then, shoot."

"I'm in Panama City, trying to catch up with an old friend. Think you can find an address for me?"

Tracy took a moment before answering, the murmurs of his colleagues filling the silence. "What's the angle?"

"Might be nothing, but he called me yesterday, said something about needing my advice. He sounded distressed. Thought I'd check up on him. Haven't gotten a hold of him today. Patience isn't my forte."

Hatch gave him Ryker's name. After a few moments, Tracy relayed the man's address. A second later, Hatch's phone alerted to an incoming message. Tracy forwarded her the info and a map display activated, showing Ryker's house was located approximately fifteen miles south of the airport, a half-hour drive at most.

"Thanks for your help," Hatch said. "I'll be in touch."

"Listen, Hatch. Don't go creating a shitstorm, all right? Need you free and clear."

"Not looking to stir things."

"You never do. Doesn't mean it's not on the radar of possibility."

"Dark clouds seem to follow. I don't control them, just handle the business end when they break wide open," Hatch said. "Plus, like I said, this is a personal visit. Doubt there's any merit to my concern."

"When you worry, I worry."

"Don't."

Tracy cleared his throat and lowered his voice to almost a whisper. "Just an FYI, we've got a situation rapidly developing at the moment. Might need you in the field sooner than later, if you're feeling up to it."

Hatch knew what Tracy was really saying. Up to it was his way of asking if she'd come to terms with Cruise's death. She doubted she ever would. Time and distance had given her perspective. Activation meant a return to the field of battle, her home away from home. She ran the prospect in her mind for a second longer before answering. "I'm ready. Let me know the when and where, and I'll be there."

"I'll keep you posted once I've got a handle on things at my end."

Tracy covered the receiver and muffled the conversation taking place in the background. Hatch remained on the line. Although she couldn't make out the words being said, she did recognize the panicked tone of their delivery. For those like Hatch and Tracy, panic wasn't common practice. She knew without knowing, whatever was happening wasn't good.

"Gotta run. Watch your six," Tracy said and ended the call.

Hatch pocketed her phone and made her way to the rental car stand, where a disinterested employee greeted her. The girl's nametag read Martha, and her eyes were rimmed with dark circles.

"I'll take anything you have," Hatch said, getting straight to the point.

Martha nodded and clicked through her computer screen. " Looks like our only option is a gray PT Cruiser."

"Sounds good to me," Hatch replied.

Martha nodded once more, her expression solemn and understanding. She pushed herself off the worn leather stool, turning to the back wall, adorned with an array of keys hanging in neat, orderly rows. The faint jingle of metal echoed throughout the small room as she sifted through the collection, her fingers seeking the one she needed. After a few moments, the distant sounds of success signaled that she had found the Cruiser's keys.

She turned back around, the keys dangling securely in her grasp. Her footsteps tapped softly against the linoleum floor as she approached the counter. Placing the keys on the countertop, she looked expectantly at Hatch, her eyes prompting payment.

Hatch, never one to favor cards, opted for cash. It left little in the way of breadcrumbs for anyone looking for her. She sorted through the various bills in her possession, her fingers counting out the required amount.

"Um, we don't normally accept cash payment. I'll have to check with the manager." Martha spun on her heels and walked over to a small office.

Hatch waited, the exact amount of change waiting in her closed palm. She passed the time by zooming in on the map Tracy had sent, getting the lay of the land. She then expanded her view in search of a nearby hotel or motel where she could stay for the night. Hatch was examining her options when the office door opened.

Martha strode out, giving Hatch a roll of her eyes. A heavy-set older man wearing a short-sleeved dress shirt with a brown tie loosened at the neck peered up at Hatch through his wire-rimmed glasses. He gave a dismissive grunt and returned to the paperwork occupying his desktop.

"Manager said it's okay as long as you leave an additional two hundred as a security deposit." Martha leaned herself over the countertop and whispered, "Sorry about that. Marty's a real asshole sometimes."

"The deposit's fine. Thanks for the assist."

"Us girls got to stick together." Martha smiled.

"Never let 'em see it get to you." Hatch scooped the keys from the counter.

"Never do." Martha counted the cash and put it aside. "Need a receipt?"

"I'm all set." Hatch gave a nod and lifted her duffle back to her shoulder.

"Oh shoot, I didn't realize you were military. There's a discount."

"I'm not. At least not anymore."

"The discount still applies."

"How much?"

Martha smiled. "Twenty percent. It'd save you sixty bucks."

"Apply the discount then." Hatch looked at the small stack of cash.

Martha separated three twenties from the pile and slid them across the counter. Hatch shook her head. "I'm good. That's for you."

Martha's mouth opened. "I can't do that."

"Sure you can. Consider it a tip for helping me out. Girl power, right?" Hatch left the money and turned toward the lot. She shot a look back at Martha, who slipped the money into the frayed pocket of her dress before placing the remaining bills into a locked drawer beneath the counter.

Hatch pressed the lock button on the key fob. A chirp echoed from the lot. Walking in the direction of the sound, she pressed it a second time until pinpointing the flashing headlights.

She tossed her bag into the trunk and entered the vehicle. The engine came to life and Hatch made her way out of the lot. She propped her phone on her thigh and followed the GPS guiding her to Ryker's home.

The radio was tuned to a country station. The song wasn't bad, but Hatch was in the mood for quiet, having been surrounded by people on all sides for most of the morning. She thought about the hurried conversation she'd had with Ryker yesterday. Bright sun danced across the windshield. In the distance, Hatch saw a cluster of dark clouds forming. *Don't cause a shitstorm.* That wasn't the plan. It never was.

She hoped her overactive mind hadn't built Ryker's distressed tone into something it wasn't. If things worked out, she'd help him out, they'd have a beer, talk up the good old days, and laugh at the conclusion Hatch had jumped to. But wishful thinking never had a home in her head. She'd always been a *hope for the best, prepare for the worst* kind of girl.

As the road stretched out before her, Hatch ran the gambit of possibilities, and not all of them were good.

# FIFTEEN

First Sergeant Calvin Hurley led his men down the familiar suburban street, each man's dress blues crisply pressed and gleaming with the precision only a Marine could achieve. The sun crept upward in the sky, the cooler morning now giving way to the heat of the day, casting the neighborhood in its soft haze. This quiet street, lined with immaculately manicured lawns and ornate gardens, would serve as the backdrop for the solemn task they had been entrusted with.

As they approached Ryker's home and exited Hurley's vehicle, he glanced at the men accompanying him. Staff Sergeant Greg Brunson, Sergeant Roger Kastner, Sergeant Mark Li, and Staff Sergeant James Woodrow stood tall and somber, their faces personifying the heaviness they felt in their hearts. They were not only there to pay their respects to a fallen brother, but also to support the family left behind by the recently deceased Gunnery Sergeant Jeff Ryker.

The door opened, revealing his tear-streaked widow. Renee Ryker's eyes, red and swollen from the weight of her loss, stared out at Hurley with a vacancy he'd seen countless times before. Beside her stood Amanda, her ten-year-old daughter, clutching a stuffed bear with a Marine Corps emblem sewn on its chest. A symbol of the father she would now only know through stories and photographs.

As each Marine stepped forward in turn, they offered condolences laced with the solemnity of a military funeral. Each man spoke from the depths of their heart, their words meant to provide some small solace in the face of unimaginable pain.

Finally, it was Hurley's turn. As he stepped forward, he looked into Renee's eyes and saw a strength that defied the depths of her sorrow. He knew that, in the days and months to come, she would need every ounce of that resilience to face the challenges ahead.

"Renee," he began, his voice steady and filled with respect. "I know there are no words that can ease the pain you and Amanda are feeling right now. But please know that Jeff was not only an exemplary Marine, but also a dear friend to all of us. We are here not only to pay our respects but also to offer our support, in any way we can."

As the other Marines nodded in agreement, Hurley took a deep breath and continued, "If you don't mind, I'd like a few moments alone with you."

Renee nodded, her eyes glistening with unshed tears as she ushered her daughter closer. The other Marines stepped outside, their collective presence a silent sentinel.

Once they were alone, Hurley knelt to Amanda's level, the weariness of his years in the Corps replaced by a soft, fatherly gaze. "Amanda, I want you to know that we'll always be here for you, and we'll make sure you never forget what a great man your father was."

He stood and faced Renee, pulling her into an embrace. For a few seconds, her body vibrated with sobs against his chest. They separated, and she guided him into the living room, wiping her cheeks and nose with a sleeve. Amanda scurried over to a desk near a bookcase, the surface covered in a variety of crayons. She sat at her makeshift artist's station and resumed coloring the sheet of paper, the act seeming to serve as an escape for the grieving child.

Hurley took a deep breath as he settled onto the couch beside Renee. Her face was stained with tracks of tears that had dried and been replaced by fresh ones. He could see the weight of her sorrow pressing down upon her, pinning her to the seat, numb.

On the end table next to her, he noticed a bottle of prescription medication and a half-filled glass of white wine providing silent company.

Hurley knew the drugs, and the wine were temporary salves, inadequate to fill the void left by her loss. But it was always worth a shot.

"I want you to know," Hurley began, the words sticking in his throat, "that I take full responsibility for what happened. In all my years of service, nearly twenty-five of them, I've never had to face something like this."

Renee's eyes, raw and red, lifted to meet his. He could see her searching for answers within his own stormy gaze, and he forced himself to continue.

"It was supposed to be a routine training demonstration, just fast-roping out of a helicopter, something we've done a million times before. Your husband was stepping out to rope down when he lost his footing." The memory played out in Hurley's mind like a film reel, torturing him with its relentless replay.

"I was my fault. I stumbled and ... bumped him. I tried to grab him. I swear I did." Hurley's voice trembled with the weight of his guilt. "But it was too late."

A new wave of tears threatened to spill from Renee's eyes, and Hurley felt his own heart constricting in his chest. He had been part of countless missions, made decisions that had saved lives and lost them, but this—this was a burden that weighed heavier than any he had shouldered before.

"I'm so sorry," he whispered, the words inadequate in the face of her pain. But as he sat there, the shadows of remorse and regret stretching out before them both, he knew that he would carry this weight for the rest of his life.

"Jeff always admired you. He told me how your steadfast faith and unwavering support carried him through his darkest days as a Marine," she said, her eyes meeting his. "You can't bear the weight of what happened alone. Every Marine knows what's at stake. It comes with the territory."

Renee continued as she laid a gentle hand on his rigid shoulders, adding her weight to the load they already carried. "If it weren't for you, I would have been widowed a long time ago," she confessed, her eyes shimmering with unshed tears. "Thank you for giving me more time with him. For saving him when you could."

As her words reached Hurley's heart, they also tore at his conscience. The truth gnawed at him—deemed a necessary evil, it did little to alleviate the burden. Renee's recollections of Ryker's trust and reverence only served to exacerbate the inner turmoil plaguing him. The weight of his actions pressed down, threatening to crush the man beneath its unforgiving force.

Hurley cleared his throat, drawing Renee's attention to the duffle bag he had brought with him. She eyed it curiously, not having noticed it before.

"May I?" Hurley asked, gesturing to the bag.

"Of course."

He unzipped the bag, revealing several stacks of cash neatly bundled inside. Renee's eyes widened at the sight of it.

"You see," Hurley began, his voice gruff but tinged with warmth. "The guys and I, we pooled our money together. We know nothing can replace Jeff, but we hope it'll help alleviate some of the financial burden."

Renee stared at the money, overwhelmed with emotion. She asked no questions as he slid it closer. Instead, she wrapped her arms around Hurley's strong frame.

"Thank you," she whispered, tears streaming down her face and mingling with the lines etched in his skin. "Thank you so much."

They separated, and Renee did her best to collect herself, wiping her eyes and taking a shaky breath.

Hurley's eyes softened, his gruff exterior melting away as he placed a hand on her shoulder. "If there's ever anything you need, Renee, don't hesitate to reach out to me or any of the others. We're here for you."

Renee only nodded.

Hurley continued to sit alongside his Marine's widow on a beige sofa in the small living room, his broad shoulders hunched. The two sat in silence, neither having any more words to spare at the moment.

A soft rustling came from the corner of the room where Amanda was bent over the piece of paper, feverishly working the crayons scattered around her. She stood and padded across the carpet, her tiny hands clutching a sheet of paper. She held it up to her mother, who took it with a trembling hand. "I made this for Daddy," she said quietly.

Hurley and Renee looked down at the crayon image. The picture depicted her late husband, clad in his Marine uniform, floating in a brilliant blue sky with angel's wings sprouting from his back. She traced a finger over the drawing, tears welling in her eyes.

Hurley felt a tightness grip his chest. Swallowing hard, he turned to Amanda and said, "Your father was a great Marine and one of the best men I ever had the pleasure of serving with." His voice was thick with emotion, but he forced the words out.

Amanda looked up at him, her eyes wide. Hurley knew his words could never replace the father she loved and lost. As Amanda's eyes began to water, threatening to spill over with tears, there was a sudden knock at the door.

Renee blinked back her tears and straightened her dress. "It's been like this since last night."

"I can tell whoever it is that now's not a good time, if you'd like?"

"No. It's fine. Like a Band-Aid, better to rip it off quickly."

Just as she was about to stand, Amanda darted for the door. "I'll get it."

Before Renee could protest, her daughter was in the hallway.

"She's the spitting image of Jeff. At least I've got her to keep me going."

Hurley didn't have the words. He prepared to leave, grabbing his cover off the coffee table in front of him.

"Won't you stay a bit longer?"

"Sure. Whatever you need." Hurley sank back into the couch and waited for the visitor to step inside.

# SIXTEEN

Detective Santiago let out a sigh of relief as she entered the precinct, her weary bones aching from a night spent on her mother's lumpy couch. The faint scent of Cuban coffee wafted through the air, a bittersweet reminder of the home she'd left behind. At least she'd managed to keep her promise to her daughter, Isabella, last night by reading her a bedtime story and tucking her in. The image of her little girl's sleepy smile brought warmth to her heart, a small moment of reprieve from the weight of the world on her shoulders.

Unlike the day before, Santiago arrived at the department on time, the pale morning light reflecting off the cold tile floor. She navigated the maze of cubicles, passing fellow officers immersed in their work, the familiar hum of copiers and phones providing a soundtrack to their daily routine. It was the calm before the storm and the part she hated most about her job. For her, the street held value. It's where she cut her teeth before being called up to the detective bureau.

As she reached her cubicle, she tossed her worn leather bag onto the chair, the brass buckles clanging against the metal frame. The sight of her cluttered desk was both comforting and overwhelming, a physical manifestation of the cases awaiting her.

Most of the pile was composed of the robbery team responsible for six major hits over the past several months. All the victims were drug dealers, which made things complicated from both sides of the house. The department didn't care much for the victims, and the victims didn't care much for the cops.

It was the seventh case that had stoked her investigative fire. But because it resulted in a double murder, the investigation was pushed off to Malcolm and, based on his investigative skill, was likely to go unsolved. Something she hoped to remedy, with or without the support of her supervisor.

One of the junior detectives occupying the cubicle opposite hers peeked his head around. "You're here early."

She cut him a look that silenced any further comments and forced the green detective into a retreat behind his partition.

No sign of Detective Malcolm, which, for Santiago, was a good thing. Maybe his late night of report writing had forced him to hit the snooze one too many times. She started walking toward the breakroom to make herself a cup of coffee, her second of the morning, when Captain Parnell stuck his head out of his office and asked to have a word with her. The look on his face told her that whatever she had coming wasn't good.

Detective Santiago stepped into the captain's office. She stood on the threshold and leaned against the door, but Parnell beckoned her inside with a stern gesture.

"Close the door behind you," he said, his voice tight and controlled. Santiago hesitated for a moment, feeling the impending unease that settled in her chest, but she obeyed.

With the door shut, she initially opted to stand, arms crossed defensively, but Parnell motioned toward the seat across from his desk. "Sit." His tone was laced with a subtle warning.

Santiago complied, and Parnell regarded her with the look a schoolteacher would give a disruptive student just prior to sending them to the principal's office.

"I thought I told you to steer clear of Detective Malcolm's investigation," he said, his gaze unwavering.

She struck a look of defiance, her chin raised in challenge. "Some investigation," she retorted. "Is that what you're calling it these days?"

Parnell's eyes darkened, and he glowered at her. "Enough, Santiago. I can't keep running interference for you every time you get a wild hair up your ass about a case."

"I never asked you to."

He leaned back in his chair, his expression softening slightly. "Drop the tough guy act. I know you're a good cop. You don't need to prove anything to me or anyone else."

"I'm not. I'm just doing my job the only way I know how."

He shook his head, disappointment evident in his eyes. "You're swimming upstream on this one. Malcolm already fired off an email to the chief requesting you stay out of the way."

A smug look crossed Santiago's face. "Maybe I should shoot the chief an email telling him he's got a moron running a double homicide."

Parnell's brow furrowed, and he slammed his hands on the desk. "Damn it, this is what I'm talking about. Cut the shit. Final warning."

"Is that all?"

Parnell took a deep breath, his jaw clenched. "For now."

Santiago stood up, her anger boiling over, and stormed out of the office. She let the door slam shut behind her, leaving Parnell to stare at the empty chair.

Santiago's eyes darted around the office. No one dared meet her glare. The breakroom was now a distant thought as she weaved her way back through the labyrinth of cubicles lining her path to her desk.

She grabbed the worn leather handle of her satchel and slung it over her shoulder. It bounced against her department-issued Glock tucked into the holster on her hip. The blood evidence from the previous night's crime scene resting inside called to her. She knew Captain Parnell had warned her, explicitly stating that she should avoid interfering with Detective Malcolm's investigation.

*Good cops don't always do what they're told. They do what's right.* It was something her father had said to her in the months prior to his death, when he'd been gunned down on duty. The killer never caught. The thought fueled the drive she put into every case. It was the same instinctual need for justice that pushed her forward now.

With a glance toward Captain Parnell's office, she strode toward the door leading to the hallway. Less than a minute later, she was greeted by a blast of warm air as she ventured forward on a path she knew she shouldn't be navigating. But there was no turning back now.

As Detective Santiago walked to her unmarked car, the clamor of the precinct faded, replaced by the steady hum of city life. Her thoughts raced, a symphony of possibilities and consequences playing out in her mind. She knew full well that defying Captain Parnell could cost her dearly, but she also knew that this case was more than just another puzzle to be solved.

She unlocked her car and slid into the driver's seat, the familiar scent of worn leather and stale coffee enveloping her. She gripped the steering wheel and started the engine.

Unzipping the satchel, she fished out her cellphone. After scrolling the list of contacts, Santiago found the number she was looking for and hit the call button. It rang twice before a male voice sounded from the other end.

"Hello?"

"Orson, it's Santiago."

"Hey stranger. Long time." Kyle Orson chuckled.

"I take it you're working today?"

"You know it. Love me some evidence processing."

"You start on the double from the other night?" Santiago hated small talk, but in this case, she indulged.

"Nah. Had a stabbing from the other week that got backlogged. Trying to play catchup before I dive into that other mess."

"Well, I'm gonna bump it up on your priority list."

"I thought Malcolm was working it. His name was on the submission forms."

"He is. I'm—um—helping."

"Sounds to me like you're doing a little moonlighting."

"Doesn't matter." Santiago's eyes gave an involuntary roll as she put the car into drive. "I've got something I need to add to the top of your pile."

"Doesn't work that way. You know that."

"It does today." She felt the frustration of another potential roadblock and decided to head it off at the pass. "You owe me. Or has that been backlogged, too?"

"Geesh. No need for hostilities." His voice now sheepish. "You know I'd do anything for you. All you have to do is ask nicely."

"I'll save my please and thank yous for when I get there." She looked at the clock. "Which should be in about twenty minutes."

"See you then." Orson ended the call.

Santiago had made her choice. She would personally deliver the blood evidence to the lab, come what may. This was her path now, and one she would see through to the end.

# SEVENTEEN

Hatch relied on her phone's GPS to guide her from the bustling airport to the address Tracy had given her for Ryker. She hadn't spent much time in the sunshine state, but during her relatively short drive, Hatch wondered if the majority of residents were retired NASCAR racers. The highways' posted speed limits seemed more a suggestion, and one that few seemed to follow. Keeping up with the flow of traffic had improved her time until she reached the backroads of the final few miles of her journey. Stop and go traffic, hindered by the seemingly endless stretch of lights she encountered, balanced out the speed of before.

Panama City was an eclectic mix. Residential and industrial zoning abutted in an indistinct pattern, blurring the lines between the two. The socioeconomic division typical of most cities and towns she'd experienced was less obvious.

She'd pass through a street of dilapidated homes and abandoned buildings to find herself in a quaint, picturesque neighborhood two blocks later. She finally made the last turn onto the street where Ryker resided.

His home was nestled in one of the more put-together neighborhoods she'd driven through thus far. The houses on this street were bigger and more lavish. Hatch was impressed. She figured military pay must go a lot farther here than in most places, or maybe Ryker's wife was the breadwinner. Hatch knew little about the woman except from what he'd told her years ago. She wondered how a surprise visit from a random female from Ryker's military past would look to his wife. The thought hadn't dawned on her until she was a few houses away.

Hatch saw something that pushed the previous thought from her mind. The sight of several Marines lingering in the yard outside the home wearing their dress uniforms gave Hatch pause. As she exited the rental car and approached, the solemn looks on their faces served to further worsen the concern growing in the pit of her stomach. She approached a large Marine Staff Sergeant with the last name Brunson etched into the nametag centered an eighth of an inch above the right breast pocket. His arm was bent across the middle of his barreled chest, held in place by a sling. He was staring at the ground and shifted his gaze to Hatch as she approached.

"Staff Sergeant," Hatch said, adding a nod of respect.

"Ma'am." His voice was deep and low, carrying a hint of southern twang. He returned Hatch's nod with a slight bow of his head. "Here to pay your respects?"

"I'm here to see Jeff Ryker." Hatch gave a second scan of the men lining the walkway to the front door. She recognized the pain, seeing in it the same grief she'd experienced far too often in her own life.

"I'm sorry. You didn't hear?" Brunson's blue eyes gleamed brightly against the mid-morning sun. A deep sadness lay just beneath.

"I spoke to him last night." Hatch's words came out in a soft mumble and were as much for her own benefit as for the Marine standing before her. "What happened?"

"Training accident. Last night."

Hatch's gut twisted. A ghost from her past was now a ghost of her present. She was at a loss.

"His wife and daughter are inside, if you'd like me to escort you in?" Brunson extended his good arm for Hatch to take. He gave a passing glance to the scar running up the right side of her arm. Unlike civilian eyes, Brunson's carried none of the judgement, showing a silent reverence of respect.

Hatch passed on the offer, the military man's pedigree apparent in his professionalism. "No need. But thank you."

Brunson nodded and then stepped aside, clearing the path for Hatch. She made her way forward along the decorative walkway lined with colorful flowers native to the warm climate. The floral notes added their natural perfume to the heavy air. Under any other circumstance, the combination would've been refreshing. But here, against the backdrop of tragedy, they only served as a reminder of the tranquility ravaged by Ryker's death.

Hatch stood on the porch, feeling sorely underdressed compared to the Marines behind her. She wore a black t-shirt neatly tucked into tan cargo pants and a pair of lightweight sand-colored combat boots, the casual wear common among military and police around the world.

She let out a long, smooth exhale, steadying herself for what waited beyond. Hatch knocked and then took a step back.

Hatch heard the pitter patter of tiny feet approaching from the other side. Her heart sank. A moment later, the door opened, and she was greeted by a little girl whose bright eyes were wet with fresh tears. The tiny face was a mirror reflection of the man she knew and seeing him in the girl only worsened the pain of his loss.

"Hi there," Hatch said, bending slightly to address the young girl. "I'm an old friend of your father. Mind if I come in?"

She gave a slow nod. Her sad eyes traced along the damaged arm of the new guest. "My mom's in the living room."

Hatch followed the little girl inside. Quiet settled as she closed the door behind her. Hatch heard the soft murmurs of conversation from the room off to the right. She came to the edge of the living room and saw Ryker's wife seated on a couch next to an older Marine in the same dress as the others outside. He bore the rank of First Sergeant. His face was grim.

"Mommy, someone's here to see you." The girl made her introduction and then scurried off to a desk littered with drawing materials. She saw Daphne in the manners and movements of the child. The thought of her niece worsened the darkness blanketing the room.

Ryker's widow made a move to stand. Hatch gave a gentle wave of her hand. "Please don't get up on my account."

She took her suggestion, seemingly grateful to remain seated. "Thank you for coming." Her voice cracked, pain seeping into each word. "Are you a friend of my husband?"

"I knew him years ago." Hatch fumbled with the words. "I'm so sorry for your loss."

"I appreciate you stopping by." She eyed Hatch with a thoughtful gaze. "I'm Renee, Jeff's wife. My apologies, but I'm not good with faces, especially under the circumstances. You are?"

"Rachel Hatch."

"Oh, Jeff's mentioned your name before. You're the runner, right?"

"I am. Your husband and I had a bit of a tug of war to see who was the fastest."

A weak smile formed at the edge of her mouth. "He said you were the fastest woman he'd come across."

"It's a good memory."

"If I remember correctly, you're in the Army?"

"Was. My service was cut short a while back." Hatch rubbed at the scar.

Renee nodded. "From what my husband told me, you were a hell of a soldier."

"The feeling was mutual. I can assure you." Hatch saw the Marine evaluating her. "Sorry for dropping in unannounced."

"Please don't." Renee looked momentarily confused. "Did you not know about Jeff's—"

Hatch saw the pain. Saying the word was a challenge in and of itself. Hatch knew it well. The memories of the fallen were easier to draw upon than the painful reminder of the tragedy that stole them. "No. I didn't."

"But you're here. Were you in town?"

Hatch shook her head no. "He called me last night. Thought I'd stop by and check in on him."

"Where from?"

"Colorado." Hatch noticed the First Sergeant perk up, taking more of an interest in the conversation. "Flew in this morning."

"You're some kind of friend to hop on a plane at the drop of a hat."

Hatch gave a shrug. "I think the First Sergeant would agree, it's like that in the brotherhood. We take care of our own."

The gruff Marine stirred and offered a solemn nod. He then stood and extended a hand in Hatch's direction. "First Sergeant Calvin Hurley. I was Gunny's supervisor here. Any friend of Jeff's is a friend of mine."

"Sorry for your loss." Hatch received the Marine's hand and exchanged a firm shake.

"God only takes the best of us. Jeff's testament to that."

Hatch nodded. She turned her attention back to Renee. "I don't mean to take up your time. I'll leave you be and let you have your space."

Renee's legs wobbled slightly as she stood. "I'm so glad you stopped by."

"I'm sorry it was under these circumstances."

"Not sure how long you plan to be in town." Renee fought back against the tears forming. "Will you be at his service? It's in a couple days."

"I'll have to see. I'm still playing catchup on all this." Hatch saw the disappointment. "I'll do my best to make it."

"I'm sure he'd like that." Renee smiled. She bent and picked up a slip of paper the size of an index card. "Here's the information on his service. If you're still around."

Hatch took the mass card and slid it into her pocket. Renee then reached out and gave Hatch a hug. "Maybe you can stop by when I'm not such a mess. I'd love to hear some stories from Jeff's past. It helps."

"I'd like that." Hatch grabbed a pen from the end table and jotted her cellphone number on a scrap of paper. She noticed a crayon drawing of a Marine with wings resting on the tabletop. It tore at the armor coating Hatch's heart, and she fought against the sensation.

Hurley escorted Hatch to the door. He opened it, the air conditioning waging a battle against the encroaching heat. "Thank you for paying your respects."

Hatch nodded but remained on the threshold a moment longer. "Could you tell me a little about what happened to Ryker?"

Hurley looked back in the direction of the living room. "Now's not the time. But maybe we can set a time to meet and discuss it later?"

"Works for me. Just trying to wrap my mind around all of this."

"We all are." Hurley scanned his Marines in the yard. "I'll grab your number from Renee and try to touch base before you go."

They exchanged another handshake before Hatch left the home. The door to Ryker's house closed behind her. The other Marines looked over. She gave a general nod to the group as she passed by on her way back to her car.

Hatch gave one final look back at the home, now broken by tragedy, and then drove away. Without Ryker to answer the questions generated by his call, Hatch wondered if she ever would know the reason he needed to speak with her. Maybe this Hurley would be able to shed some light. Her gut told her it was worth the effort.

As a military police officer, it had long been her role to speak for the dead. Hatch set her mind to doing just that. But first, she needed to find a place to stay if she planned on sticking around for a few days.

# EIGHTEEN

NCIS AGENT BEAU GRANGER SAT AT HIS DESK, HUNCHED OVER THE REPORT detailing the events of the previous night. A small, dim lamp cast long shadows across the room, providing just enough light for him to scrutinize the document. It was the kind of night that Granger hated, the inescapable weight of his responsibilities heavy on his shoulders.

Gunnery Sergeant Jeff Ryker's lifeless face stared up at him from the pages, a painful reminder of the tragedy that had occurred during a routine helicopter fast-roping demonstration. The words in the report seemed to blur together, but Granger knew them all too well. Ryker had failed to gain a proper hold on the rope before making his descent, resulting in a fatal fall from the helicopter's skid, one hundred feet to the unforgiving concrete tarmac below. He was dead on impact.

Granger's fingers danced across the keyboard, adding the necessary edits and final touches to the report. The incident was deemed an accident, and the blame would be placed solely on Ryker's shoulders. Granger's heart raced, conflicting emotions battling within him. His professional side insisted that he submit the report—it was his duty, after all—but another part of him resisted, begging him to reconsider.

He reread the statements given by the members of the Marine demo team. His eyes came to rest on the last one, written by the unit's top dog,

First Sergeant Calvin Hurley, a man Granger had known for most of his life. The initial wording noted the specifics of the training demonstration, documenting time, location, and conditions of the incident. The boiler plate language included in all such reports was consistent with all the other members' descriptions. It was the latter part, the section documenting Hurley's final moments with Ryker, that gave Granger pause.

*Gunnery Sergeant Ryker, one of the finest soldiers I've had the honor to serve with, stood on the skid to my immediate right.*

*The chopper was suddenly jolted by a violent gust of wind that tossed us like ragdolls. In the wake of the turbulence, I found myself struggling to maintain my footing. My arm flailed wildly, connecting with Ryker and knocking him off balance. The result of the impact cost him to lose his grip on the rope—his lifeline.*

*My instincts kicked in, and my hand shot out to grasp him. I watched Ryker give way. Gunnery Sergeant Ryker fell to the tarmac below.*

*The consequences of this horrific incident bear down on me like a crushing vice. The memory of Ryker's fall haunts my every waking moment, a constant reminder of the life I failed to save. I cannot express the depth of my sorrow, and the agony that fills me as I think of the void left in the hearts of those who loved him. May he rest in peace, and may I find the strength to carry on in his memory.*

*I submit this statement, acknowledging my role in this tragedy. Any resulting consequence from this incident rests squarely on me.*

Like a good Marine, and any battle-tested commander, First Sergeant Hurley's acknowledgement of his actions and assumption of responsibility were commensurate with the type of man Granger knew him to be. Regardless of the resulting consequences, nothing in his statement warranted prosecution. It would be listed as a training accident, and the investigation would be closed as such.

The thought of the potential fallout from Hurley's admission of guilt would have long-ranging repercussions for the decorated Marine's future. Granger assigned a redaction clause to the statement, ensuring that nothing disclosed would be released without his consent. This would protect his friend. He owed Hurley that much. Debts incurred often carried a price. Granger accepted his.

As his finger hovered over the 'submit' button, Granger closed his eyes, attempting to find solace in the darkness. A single bead of sweat rolled down his forehead, a testament to the turmoil brewing within. He took a deep breath, steeling himself for the decision he was about to make.

With a heavy heart and a shaking hand, Granger clicked the button. The report was submitted, Ryker's death marked as a tragic accident. Granger's eyes remained closed. The consequences of this decision would haunt him, the guilt slowly consuming him from the inside out. But for now, he would keep his secret hidden, tucked away in the darkest corners of his soul.

Only time would reveal the true cost of his actions, and when that day came, Beau Granger would be forced to confront the demons he had created. Until then, he would carry on in the name of duty and loyalty.

His phone line lit up, followed by a call from the front desk. He picked up the receiver, cradling it against his neck as he fished out the pack of cigarettes from the top drawer. He slapped the top of the pack against the palm of his hand several times before stripping away the plastic seal. "Abby, do me a favor and tell 'em I just sent it."

"It's not command. It's a reporter from the local paper looking for a quote."

"Great." Granger grunted. He shook one of the cigarettes loose, and it rolled across his desk, coming to rest against the photograph of the dead Marine. "Not in the mood."

"Is that what you want me to tell them?" Abby asked.

His secretary had been working at the base in that capacity for many years prior to Granger's arrival a year ago and would likely be sitting at the same desk for many more after his departure. Until that time, he resigned himself to the fact that Abigail Kudrow ran the roost, and he was just another hen in the coop.

"Put 'em through." Granger closed the file folder and the image of the dead Marine disappeared behind the manilla covering.

"Hello?" A female voice asked from the other end.

"This is Agent Granger. How may I be of assistance?"

"My names Deborah Cantrell, I'm with the Pensacola Voice. It's my understanding you're the investigating authority on the death that occurred on base late yesterday."

"I am."

"Just wanted to see if I could obtain a comment."

"It's currently under review."

Cantrell released an audible sigh of frustration. "I'm on a deadline."

"Sounds like your problem." Granger rolled the cigarette between his fingers, the nicotine calling to him.

"Can I level with you?" Without allowing time for a response, Cantrell continued, "I'm new here. Not to journalism. Just to Panama City. This is my first real story. I don't want to fire off an article that doesn't do justice to the serviceman who lost his life."

"Admirable. But I'm not at liberty to discuss the incident."

"I get it. Truly, I do." Cantrell softened her tone. "My husband served."

"And you think that somehow qualifies me to break rank? I'm sure your husband can fill you in on how things work."

"He could if he were still alive."

"Didn't mean any disrespect."

"None taken. He lost his life last year three weeks before his deployment was up." She choked on the words. "I'm not looking for favors. Just trying to keep things afloat on my end. I've been left holding the bag and can't run the risk of losing my first gig."

"I can't go into the specifics. That's outside my authority. What I can tell you is that Gunnery Sergeant Riker's death is being ruled accidental."

"Can you tell me if he has any surviving family members?"

"He leaves behind a wife and child."

"They've got a hard road ahead. I can attest to that."

"Everyone does." Granger felt the early morning Florida sunlight piercing the window blinds and beginning its daily assault on his office's air conditioning.

"Can I quote you?"

"Just keep it simple. And don't make me regret our conversation."

"Thank you."

"Don't mention it." Granger dropped the receiver back into its cradle and pushed back from his desk.

He tucked the cigarette behind his ear and walked the file folder over to the metal cabinet on the far side of his office. After locking away the hardcopy, he grabbed the pack off his desk and headed for the door. It was going to be one of those days where one smoke wouldn't be enough to take the edge off.

On his way out, Abby looked up from her desk. She gave him a questioning look. "Thought you quit for good last time?"

"Nobody likes a quitter," Granger muttered.

"Guess you've got your reasons." Abby resumed her tasks without adding anything further.

Granger paused by the door, briefly taking in the last bit of cool air before stepping out into the muggy early morning sun. He exited and strode away from the main entrance to a corner designated for smoking.

As he pulled the cigarette from his ear, he thought about Abby's parting words. She couldn't have been more right. Closing the Ryker file brought with it a burden of responsibility he hadn't felt in a long time, the weight of which stretched far beyond that of the thick case file he'd just laid to rest.

# NINETEEN

DETECTIVE SANTIAGO HEADED TO THE BAY COUNTY MEDICAL EXAMINER'S office located on the west side of Panama City near Goose Bayou. Santiago exited her vehicle and was struck by the strong smell of fish carried by the breeze. She entered the cool air-conditioned main lobby, the temperature-controlled space replacing the foul odor of the outside with a medicinal scent.

She walked to the receptionist manning the front desk, a pleasant woman named Blanche Montrose. Santiago had crossed paths with her numerous times over the course of her career. They kept the banter light, neither pushing for anything beyond small talk.

"Hey, Blanche, can you buzz Orson? He's expecting me."

"Let me see if I can reach him." Montrose shifted with the economy of movement equivalent to a three-toed sloth. She dialed the extension and played with the phone cord while she waited. A couple seconds later, Montrose connected and said, "Your favorite is here." She looked up in Santiago's direction. "On his way."

Orson's polished leather shoes echoed across the pristine marble floor of the main lobby as he entered through the restricted access door. The white lab coat draped over his tall frame swished softly with each step.

The corners of his mouth twitched into a friendly smile when he spotted Santiago, but the annoyance lurking in his eyes betrayed his true feelings.

"Detective Santiago," Orson greeted, extending a hand for a firm handshake. "Always a pleasure."

Santiago's grin was mischievous. "You know, Orson, you could try to sound more convincing."

"You know I can't process evidence out of order. My director would have my head if he knew." Orson sighed, his annoyance becoming more pronounced.

Santiago's grin morphed into a smirk as she leaned in. "And you would have a DUI charge if it weren't for me, remember?"

Orson's cheeks flushed a deep red as he recalled the humiliating night when he'd been stopped by a uniformed patrol officer, facing the terrifying prospect of a DUI charge. His only lifeline had been Santiago, who had swooped in like an avenging angel, talked down the officer, and driven him home.

"All right, all right," he grumbled, his embarrassment making him squirm. "How long are you going to hold that over my head?"

Santiago held up her hands in mock surrender. "Last time, I promise."

The words seemed to appease Orson enough, and he finally relented. "Fine," he said, his tone resigned, but not without warmth. "I'll take a look at the blood sample. But if my director finds out—"

"Don't worry, Orson," Santiago interrupted with a reassuring pat on the shoulder. "Your secret is safe with me."

Santiago stood in the sterile lobby of the crime lab. She reached into the satchel slung over her shoulder and pulled out the small container housing the precious blood sample recovered from the crime scene. She needed answers, and she needed them fast.

Orson, an experienced lab technician with a penchant for unraveling the mysteries of the human genome, received Santiago's offering. He slipped the sample into the breast pocket of his lab coat and offered a conflicted smile.

"I appreciate what you're doing for me on this. I really do."

"Where was it taken?" Orson asked.

"Outside the stairwell of the apartment where the double homicide took place," Santiago replied, her voice flat and emotionless.

"Why are you submitting it?" Orson's eyebrows knitted together in confusion. "Isn't Detective Malcolm the investigating officer?"

Santiago's eyes narrowed. Her lips pursed for a moment before responding. "Malcolm didn't collect it. I did."

"And why do you think it's important?"

"Call it a hunch." She leaned in closer, her voice barely above a whisper. "Just run the DNA test and call my cell if you get a return. Might be the piece that breaks this thing wide open and helps to bring some very dangerous people to justice."

Orson hesitated, searching Santiago's face for a clue to her unorthodox methods. She knew there was another reason he was helping her, an unspoken but often hinted at one that went beyond the boundaries of their professional relationship. He harbored a crush on Santiago, and had so for years, but she had always deftly sidestepped his advances. Although it hadn't stopped him from trying.

"What are you up to later?" he asked, his voice a mix of curiosity and subtle longing.

"I've got some things I need to follow up on." Santiago flashed him a polite smile, her eyes betraying the weariness of a detective consumed by her work. "Duty calls."

Orson accepted her dodging, even if a bit reluctantly, and the two exchanged goodbyes, Orson promising to notify her the moment he had anything and Santiago vowing to keep her promise by letting go of the leverage she'd been holding over him.

Santiago slipped into her sedan, wrinkling her nose against the insistent odor of stale fish continuing to cling to the muggy air. She took a deep breath, grateful for the cleaner air inside her vehicle. Starting the engine, she allowed herself a moment to savor the satisfaction of knowing the blood evidence was secure.

The sky was coated in a thick haze as Santiago navigated the familiar streets back to the precinct. Her mind raced, eager to meet with Officers Baxter and Green once they arrived for the afternoon roll call. It was crucial to compare their boot prints to the one she'd found in the blood sample. If they didn't match, it would confirm her suspicions. It would also mean Santiago was rolling with the best lead she'd had since first beginning her relentless pursuit of the elusive, and now deadly, robbery crew.

Despite the promising evidence, Santiago couldn't shake the nagging feeling that something was off. Malcolm's resistance to the idea gnawed at her thoughts. She knew they had their personal differences, but this was different. His lack of interest in the blood evidence seemed more than just obstinance—it felt deliberate.

As she parked her car and walked toward the precinct, her heart tightened with each step. The unthinkable crept into her mind: Could Malcolm be connected to the crew? It was an ugly thought, one she didn't want to entertain, but the possibility hovered at the edge of her awareness. The robbery crew had evaded capture for six months, and now she couldn't help but wonder if someone on the inside had been tipping them off.

The detective bureau buzzed as Santiago entered. She strode with purpose, the weight of her badge, and the pull of justice it carried, heavy on her hip. She looked around, Parnell was out of his office. No sign of Malcolm either. Santiago plopped into her seat. She uploaded the images from her cellphone onto her computer. She enlarged the photos of the bloody boot print, analyzing the pattern imprinted and preserved in the dried reddish brown.

She looked at the clock. Time crawled forward as she waited for the patrolmen to start their shift. Santiago then looked at a note she'd scribbled on her desktop calendar. Parent teacher conference. The time was an issue. Her mother would have to pick up Isabella from school. Santiago would have to hit warp speed to make it in time for the meeting. The constant battle for balance already seemed to be getting the best of her today.

She pushed the self-loathing away for the moment, focusing her attention back to the images on her screen. As Santiago played out the next steps in her unsanctioned investigation, the thought crept in again, approaching from the far recesses of her mind. If Malcolm was involved, she needed proof. Throwing conjecture about another cop could only be brought to light with hard evidence to back it, and even then, it would still be a potential landmine fraught with danger.

Regardless of the outcome, in that moment, Santiago made a silent vow that she would put an end to the robberies and the violence surrounding them, no matter the cost.

# TWENTY

HATCH DROVE INTO THE HEART OF PANAMA CITY. SHE HAD AN IDEA OF what she was looking for and recognized it when she saw it. A sign advertised an off-the-beaten-path motel just up the road. Hatch decided to check it out and followed the directions. Two things she immediately liked about the place were that the motel accepted cash, as evident by the sign in the manager's window, and it was a short walk from a mom-and-pop diner just down the road.

The parking lot had only two cars occupying it, one of which likely belonged to the manager or attendant. Cracked asphalt lined the sun-bleached surface in weeds of various heights. To some, maybe even most, the conditions of the rest spot's exterior would be off-putting. To Hatch, it was anything but. The anonymity it provided called to her like a siren steering a ship into jagged rocks.

She parked outside the office and stepped inside. No air conditioning cooled the room. Instead, an oscillating fan in the far corner blew the mugginess around with reckless abandon. Hatch felt sweat beginning to form. She approached the counter. The seat on the other side was vacant. A tattered index card was taped to the base of a bell, telling customers to ring for the manager. Hatch did exactly as the note instructed.

The bell didn't ring. It was more of a metallic thud. But the muted tone still did the trick. Hatch heard a man groan from the back room. Sight unseen, Hatch guessed her arrival had interrupted someone's siesta.

A tall, thin Black man emerged with a head blanketed in curly tufts of white with a matching goatee. His eyes were friendly enough. It was the expression on his face that called to question his opinion of Hatch's presence.

"Can I help you, miss?" His voice was deep. The man's words rolled out like molasses from a jar, each delivered with reverential purpose. "Need directions?"

"No, thanks. I think I'm right where I'm supposed to be." Hatch offered a smile. "I need a room."

The man seemed taken aback. "I can oblige." He shook his head and smiled in return. "Don't get much in the way of traffic these days. People want something bigger and better."

"As long as the bed's got a mattress and the room's clean, I'll be happy."

"I can vouch for both those things. Clean it myself."

"Well then, it sounds like you've got yourself a guest."

"How long d'ya plan on stickin' around?"

"Not sure yet. At least for the night." Hatch noticed a hint of disappointment flutter across the man's eyes. "Nothing's in stone at the moment. Might end up being a couple days, depending. If it's okay by you, I'd prefer to pay by the day."

"Makes the best kinda sense to me."

Hatch reached into her pocket. "I prefer to pay in cash, if that's agreeable?"

"Sign says so. And I'm the one who wrote it. Guess that makes it right as rain."

"What's the damage?"

"Be fifty-two dollars." His face cringed. "I'm sorry about the cost. Used to be less when business was better."

"Fifty-two is more than fine by me." Hatch flipped open the wad of cash, counting out the requested amount before setting it on the counter.

"Name's Carl, but people 'round here just call me Oak." He gave a sheepish grin. "As account of my height."

"Well, Oak, it's a pleasure. People usually call me Hatch."

"Is that some type of bird reference?"

"Nope. Just my last name." Both Hatch and Oak broke into a soft chuckle at that.

Oak grabbed a key off the rack behind him. "Room number seven. Best one. Plus, it's on the far side of the lot, which means you don't gotta listen to traffic passin' by all hours of the night."

"Sounds perfect." Hatch took the key. "Thank you. And I'll keep you posted on how long I plan to be in town."

"Sure thing. Stay as long as you like."

Hatch was turning to leave when Oak said, "Forgot to mention. Jimmy's Diner's just a hop an' a skip from here. Not sure your pleasure, but it's got the best damn turtle pie I've ever had."

"As long as they don't use actual turtles." Hatch followed with a wink, which forced another chuckle out of the tall, kind-hearted motel owner. She also noted that he never cast an eye of judgement at the sight of her scarred arm. As she walked out of the office, Hatch decided she liked Oak.

He hadn't lied about the room. Although lacking in amenities, everything inside was well kept and clean. Hatch set her duffle on a small wooden table. She sat on the corner of the bed. The mattress was worn but firm enough. The sheets were neatly tucked, the tight folds had precision forty-five-degree angles, leaving little doubt in Hatch's mind that the older man had once served.

Hatch took a moment to reflect on the unexpected outcome of her visit. Of all the possibilities she'd entertained since first receiving Ryker's call, his death was not even a consideration. Faced with the reality of that circumstance, it was unlikely she'd ever get to the bottom of why he'd called her.

As she pondered her next move, Hatch's stomach rumbled. She decided to take Oak's recommendation. As she stepped out, the sun broke through the morning's haze. The rays added to the climbing heat index.

Hatch bypassed her rental car, using the walk to clear her mind. She wondered if her judgment was off. Ever since Cruise had died and Savage had moved on, she felt untethered. Hatch felt she hadn't only lost them, but a part of herself, too. She accepted the possibility her decision to come here may have been a misguided attempt to resurrect the Hatch of her past, to find her next fight. The battlefield responsible for forging her character, serving as a cornerstone in her sense of self, had changed. It had once before. After getting discharged, Hatch drifted for a time until she found a way to keep moving forward.

As she walked along the edge of the road leading away from the motel, Hatch wondered if she'd find her way again. She took the slow rise in the road. Coming to the top, Hatch looked at Jimmy's Diner. The discomfort she internalized would, for the moment, have to be suppressed by a good meal. And just maybe, a piece of turtle pie.

As she pushed open the door, a cheerful chime announced her arrival. The warm, welcoming aroma of pancakes, sizzling bacon, and sweet maple syrup enveloped her. Hatch's stomach growled audibly, her brain sending a clear message that it was high time for a hearty meal. She glanced to her left and spotted a neat stack of newspapers on a small, polished table. Snatching the top copy, she surveyed the diner, noting that all the tables were occupied. Not to be deterred, she settled for a seat at the retro, fifties-style bar.

A cheerful waitress approached, deftly placing a drink napkin and a set of silverware wrapped in a crisp cloth on the counter before Hatch. "Do you need any time to look at the menu?" she asked, her voice lilting with the enthusiasm of youth. She appeared to be in her late teens or early twenties, with cheeks that hadn't yet fully settled into the angular prominence of adulthood. Her tanned skin was dotted with a constellation of freckles, and her dark hair was swept back into a casual, low ponytail. A small nametag pinned to her uniform read, "Louise."

Hatch glanced briefly at the menu before shaking her head. "That's all right," she replied with a warm smile. "I'll take whatever plate has the most food on it. And a coffee, please."

Louise flashed a warm smile at Hatch, her nimble fingers peeling the menu off the counter with effortless skill. She shot off like a bullet, her energy contagious, only to return in a flash with a steaming pot of coffee. The fragrant aroma of the hot brew wafted up to Hatch's nose as Louise poured the rich, dark liquid into the empty mug on the bar, the steam rising like a ghostly apparition.

With a grateful nod, Hatch acknowledged Louise's kind gesture, her focus now turning to the newspaper spread out before her. The headline read: Tragedy Strikes During Training Demonstration. It went on to vaguely describe the incident revolving around the death of her good friend. Hatch knew the details of an investigation would be held back from the media as long as possible. The military didn't like civilian interference and despised when they got their information wrong. Most of what was released would be limited and full of redactions. "Ryker's Death" etched in bold letters leapt off the page. She thought of Renee and her daughter.

She perused the article, her gaze focusing on a quote from NCIS Agent Beau Granger, the investigating officer who had responded to the scene of the tragedy. "I can't say much since this is an open investigation," he stated. "All we know right now is that this was a training incident. A man lost his grip and fell. No one was able to catch him in time. I'll provide an update if I have any further information. My heart goes out to the family that Gunnery Sergeant Ryker left behind as well as his fellow Marines who feel his loss greatly."

She took a sip of the coffee, relishing the rich, bold flavor that danced on her tongue. Hatch jotted down the name "Beau Granger" on a napkin, a shrewd move that could prove valuable in the future. Hatch continued to leaf through the newspaper, her eyes dancing across the printed words that covered a variety of local topics—politics, education, sports, and weather.

As she reached the back of the newspaper, a gruesome story caught her attention. It detailed the tragic deaths of a father and his teenage son, both gunned down in their apartment. The story summarized a double murder that occurred the night before Ryker's death during which a father, Winslow Greer, known as Willie G., age 35, and his son, Winslow Jr. Greer, or JR, age 16, were killed in what investigators were saying appeared to be a drug- or gang-related homicide. The article went on to extrapolate on the long criminal history of the father, painting an all-too-familiar picture of the toll drugs play in the destruction of so many lives.

Louise's return, carrying a plate heaped with a steaming hot breakfast, interrupted Hatch's thoughts. She had set aside the newspaper and her coffee, anticipating the arrival of her requested feast. As the waitress gently placed the plate on the table, a mouthwatering assortment greeted Hatch: fluffy pancakes, crispy bacon, juicy sausage links, golden hash browns, and perfectly scrambled eggs. To complete the meal, Louise set a pot of rich maple syrup beside the plate.

Hatch couldn't help but notice the younger woman's gaze drifting toward the newspaper. "Such a shame, but it was a long time coming," she remarked, her voice tinged with a mixture of pity and resignation.

"How do you figure?" Hatch inquired, her curiosity piqued.

"My Aunt Sophia lives in that complex. Truth be told, right across the hall from those two," the girl explained, crossing her arms and furrowing her brow as she nodded toward the photograph of the now-deceased father and son drug dealers. "She used to share all kinds of horror stories with me, just based on what she'd heard through the walls. The people coming at all times of the night. The addicts lining the stairwell she had to push past with her children to get them off to school. Just terrible, ya know?"

Hatch nodded. "Sounds like a rough life. As bad as this sounds, at least it looks as though your aunt won't have to worry about that anymore."

"Someone's just gonna take his place. Never ends." Louise's expression darkened. "But that's the thing. Since the murders, I haven't been able to contact my aunt."

"Is that out of character?"

She shrugged. "I'm busy here at the diner. Working doubles a lot of the time. Tryin' to keep things afloat. I tried calling a bunch after the murders but couldn't get a hold of her. Starting to get worried is all."

"I'd be willing to see what I can do to help."

"You'd do that for me?" The young waitress' eyes watered a bit. "Why help someone you don't know?"

"I know good people when I see them. It just makes sense to help if I can." Hatch gave a smile. "I have a knack for finding people."

"Are you an investigator or something?" Louise asked.

"Something like that." Hatch grabbed a pen and napkin from the table, poised to jot down the information. "Just need your aunt's address."

Louise provided the information and left Hatch to enjoy her meal. The food served as comfort for the morning's tumultuous beginnings. She walked back to her motel room and made plans for checking out Sophia's apartment later. In the interim, she decided to get in a quick nap. A good soldier powers down when the opportunity presents, knowing the next battle may be just around the corner. As Hatch drifted off to sleep, she wondered if these old habits would ever die off or whether she would be compelled to adhere to them for the rest of her life.

# TWENTY-ONE

D<small>ETECTIVE</small> M<small>ARIBEL</small> S<small>ANTIAGO GLANCED AGAIN AT THE CLOCK, ITS TICKING</small> seeming to taunt her. 3:30 PM was rapidly approaching, and Officers Baxter and Green were still nowhere in sight. With her foot tapping impatiently, she stood in the hallway outside the roll call room, straining to hear the drone of the patrol sergeant as he went through the night's briefing.

The word 'brief' seemed like a cruel joke at this point.

Santiago's nerves were frayed, and her anxiety gnawed at her insides as she checked her watch for the umpteenth time. Time was slipping through her fingers like sand, and she could see herself being late to Isabella's parent-teacher conference. The very thought made her heart clench in frustration.

Reluctantly, Santiago pulled out her cellphone, her thumb hovering over the call button. She could ask her mother for help, but the mere idea of it felt like an admission of defeat. Already, she'd had to call her to pick up Isabella, and now this. It was as if she was stacking one failure on top of another, and it weighed heavily on her chest.

As she stood there, torn between her duty and her family, the door to the roll call room burst open, releasing a cacophony of chairs scraping against linoleum and the chatter of fellow officers. They all seemed so carefree and jovial, unaware of the storm brewing in Santiago's mind.

Her eyes scanned the crowd, searching for Baxter and Green, the only two people who could help her salvage the day. Santiago leaned against the wall outside the roll call room, her arms folded as she waited for the shift to disperse. Officers Baxter and Green exchanged glances as they exited the room, their eyes meeting hers.

Green gave a subtle nod and said, "Heard you needed to see us? Something wrong?"

Santiago could see their defenses rise, likely assuming they'd made a mistake, and she was there to reprimand them. It wasn't an uncommon occurrence, so their initial reaction was justified. However, in this case, it was unwarranted.

"No problem," Santiago said, her voice steady. "Just wanted to follow up with you guys about the double homicide from yesterday."

Baxter and Green visibly relaxed. "Go ahead, shoot," Baxter replied, his voice casual.

"You two were first on scene, correct?" Santiago asked, her dark eyes scrutinizing them.

"That's right," Green replied, his tone guarded. "We wrote a supplemental report documenting our actions."

"I know. I read it."

"It was a thorough report. Signed off on. Is there an issue?" Green's question had an edginess to it, the senior of the two officers taking a protective tone.

Shaking her head, Santiago replied, "No issue. Just trying to fit a piece of evidence in and make sure I have it correct."

The two patrolmen exchanged puzzled looks. Santiago pulled out her phone, displaying the image of the boot print she'd found in the dried blood on the external stairwell leading to the second-floor apartment where the murder took place. "Are you guys wearing the same boots you had on the night of the murders?"

Both officers nodded, their movements slightly out of sync.

"Mind if I do a quick comparison?" Santiago asked. Baxter and Green lifted each boot in turn, allowing Santiago to inspect the treads. When she finished, she released the last boot with a sigh.

Green cocked his head, a bemused smile tugging at the corner of his mouth. "So, are we the Cinderella you're looking for, or what?"

Santiago shook her head. "Doesn't look like it."

The two patrolmen exchanged glances. Baxter frowned. "What's that mean?"

Santiago shrugged, furrowing her brow. "Not sure, exactly. Would've been a lot easier if it'd been one of you. The boot tread is likely from a tactical boot. The fact it didn't come from you two makes me question who we're actually dealing with on this one."

Green's eyes widened a bit. "You thinking these guys are pros?"

"Don't know," Santiago admitted. "But one thing's for certain—they've managed to elude capture for this long, and that makes me question a whole bunch of things." She shook her head, trying to dispel the chilling implications. "Thanks, fellas. I better let you get out on the street."

The two patrolmen nodded and started down the hall toward the door leading to the lot where the patrol vehicles were parked. Santiago followed, quickening her steps as she neared her car.

Green called to her across the lot. "Hey, Santiago, I thought Malcolm was heading the case?"

Santiago had a plethora of responses she could offer, many laden with expletives about her opinion of her colleague. Instead, she chose the simplest answer, albeit a lie that carried a thread of truth. "I'm assisting."

The patrolmen turned, their attention shifting to their pre-shift vehicle inspections. Santiago slid into her car, her mind racing with the unanswered questions that now haunted the case.

Santiago sat behind the wheel of her department-issued sedan, the tires screeching as she sped out of the parking lot. She glanced at her watch, her heart sinking at the realization that she was already late for the parent-teacher conference. Her only hope now was to arrive before the teacher had left for the day.

As Santiago's sedan tore through the streets, her mind raced through a myriad of possibilities that her recent discovery might have on the investigation. Captain Parnell's reaction weighed heavily on her thoughts, but there was another person who might be able to shed light on her findings —White.

The neighbor, who Santiago suspected had witnessed some aspect of the grisly murder, had been unwilling to talk initially. Now that some time had passed, Santiago wondered if the woman's resolve might have weakened. After the conference, she'd pay her a visit. It meant delaying her return home, but as she weighed the potential fallout within her personal life against the objective, the decision was clear.

With a deep breath, Santiago placed the call she'd been dreading. Her mother, Rosa, answered on the third ring. Santiago's voice was strained as she explained that she needed to check one more thing before heading home after the conference.

As expected, Rosa gave her a ration of crap about being late to the conference, which quickly escalated to an argument about Maribel's inability to make it home in time for dinner. Santiago gritted her teeth, accepting her mother's rebuke, and promised to do her best to make it home on time.

Rosa didn't believe her.

The precarious balance between her personal life and her commitment to the case was threatening to topple, the case slowly tipping the scale in its direction. Santiago knew all too well the price she might have to pay, but the pursuit of justice was relentless, and she couldn't afford to let it slip through her fingers.

# TWENTY-TWO

HATCH EASED HER RENTAL PT CRUISER TO A STOP A DISCREET DISTANCE from the weathered facade of Sophia's apartment complex. Her belly filled with the warm embrace of Jimmy's Diner's finest, the engine purred to silence when she killed the ignition, her gaze trained on the building before her.

Hatch was a seasoned soldier, and she knew better than most the importance of easing into a new environment. She likened the urban jungle before her to the deserts and forests where she had developed her skills, one of them being surveillance. She settled into this new location, embracing the natural order of her surroundings.

It wasn't long before she noted a group of young men loitering near the entrance. Their attire was distinctive, a sea of matching colors marking them as potential members of a local gang. Though Hatch couldn't pin down their specific affiliation, she knew that gangs thrived in the harsh underbelly of cities like this one.

Their presence carried with it a high potential for trouble, and as Hatch sat watching, she wondered if somehow Sophia White had stumbled into their path. Sophia's disappearance and the presence of a gang in the area was an unsettling prospect. Hatch couldn't ignore the possibility.

Hatch exited the car, her boots connecting with the pavement as her senses came alive. The city breathed around her, the cacophony of distant sirens and barking dogs a soundtrack to her pursuit.

Her muscles tensed, ready for action as Hatch's keen eyes swept the area. The sun beat down on the barren asphalt. A warm breeze cut through the apartment complex, rattling a chain link fence serving as a boundary along the property line.

The gangbangers she'd been tracking glanced her way as she approached. Their eyes, cold and calculating, bore into her, trying to decipher her purpose and, more importantly, whether she was a cop. They weren't far off the mark.

She was something else now. A specter, a ghost haunting the space between the world she knew and the one in which she now existed. Whatever conclusion the street thugs had made, it compelled them to move along. One of them spat on the ground while making direct eye contact with Hatch. She ignored the man's challenge and continued, moving between the apartment buildings. The stairwell between the two stucco buildings stretched upward to the second-floor apartment where Sophia resided.

Ascending the stairs, she took note of the dried blood, a dark stain on the gray concrete. It was a grim reminder of the violence that had unfolded only days before. A shred of police tape clung to the apartment railing above, a tattered witness to the chaos that had occurred.

The muted hues of sun filtered between the buildings, casting a somber light across the narrow corridor. The air was heavy with the memories of struggle, and the silence that now enveloped the place seemed to hold its breath, anticipating the next moment of tragedy.

She reached the second-floor landing and bypassed the apartment where the double homicide had taken place. Hatch walked over to the door across from it. She listened briefly while standing quietly outside on the landing. No sounds came from within.

Hatch knocked. She then stepped back from the door and to the left. Old habits die hard. Entrance to any unknown is considered a fatal funnel by those in both military and police tactical circles. No response came from the other side.

Hatch made another effort to listen, stepping forward and, this time, pressing her ear closer to the slight gap between the frame and the door itself. There was no movement from inside, no scurrying feet or hushed whispering. Hatch delivered a more forceful second attempt. She struck the heel of her balled fist against the hollow core wooden door. Three raps on the door echoed along the landing. Still no response from the other side.

Hatch was about to depart when she noticed why the door had a slight separation. Several pry marks scarred both the edge of the door and its frame in and around the lock. She bent and took a closer look. Saw bits of yellow in the grooves cut into the wood.

She scraped her fingernail across one of the indents. A fleck of paint clung to the tip of her finger, her suspicion confirmed. Could've been police? The thought was discarded as soon as it entered her mind. It was unlikely police would breach the door of a witness. Hatch was now left with two choices, walk away or enter. Hatch didn't know how to walk away, so the decision was clear.

Hatch looked around. Seeing the coast was clear, she pulled her military ID from her pocket. The card was the perfect blend of rigidity and flexibility. Hatch slid it into the gap. It took her no time at all before she had disengaged the lock. She felt the knob give and pushed the door open. Hatch slipped inside, quickly closing the door behind her.

The interior was dark. The shades were drawn. The only light came through the slits in the blinds. It was enough to clearly see into the apartment. Hatch quietly announced her presence. She was here to find Sophia, not scare her half to death. She called again. Hearing no response, Hatch crept deeper into the apartment.

She looked in the kitchen. Bowls of mac and cheese were set on the small oval table. The cheese had congealed, and the pasta had regained its hard, precooked consistency. She walked to the back bedroom. Drawers were pulled, clothing scattered about. She got that tingle again but didn't allow her mind to jump right into a worst-case scenario.

She ran the gambit of possibilities. One of the simpler ones she postulated was that Sophia, fearing for the safety of her children, packed up that night after the shooting. She probably would've been more open to it if it hadn't been for the mac and cheese. It sent a red flag. She decided there was something more afoot, and figuring out what that was would be the challenge.

Hatch turned to leave. Her hand was reaching for the knob when she heard footsteps. She waited for them to pass. The light slipping under the door was cast in shadow. Someone was now standing on the other side. The only thing separating her from the unknown was a hollow core wooden door.

# TWENTY-THREE

HATCH'S INSTINCTS KICKED IN AS SHE SHIFTED HER WEIGHT TO THE BALLS OF her feet, preparing to exit and face the person on the other side. She took a moment to inhale deeply, bringing her heart rate under control and her mind into focus.

She stepped out of Sophia's apartment and nearly into the fist of a Hispanic woman wearing a white button-down shirt and slacks. As Hatch prepared to counter this woman's movements, she caught a glimpse of the gun and badge on her hip.

Hatch stopped her advance, opening her fists and slowly raising her hands as the detective brought hers to her hip line. The plain clothes detective's right hand gripped her Glock. Hatch noticed the detective had flicked the retention strap forward, freeing the gun for removal from the hard plastic holster. The fact the detective hadn't drawn the weapon told Hatch she was evaluating the threat but controlled her reaction to it. In that split second, Hatch surmised the cop standing before her was no rookie.

"Detective Santiago, Panama City PD." Her voice was commanding while maintaining control. The detective's brown eyes scrutinized Hatch, conveying a mix of curiosity and caution. "Keep your hands where I can see them."

Hatch did as instructed, leaving them up in the halfway point between her midline and shoulders. "My name is Rachel Hatch. I've been asked by a relation of Miss Sophia to look into her disappearance. I'm no threat."

"I'll determine that, got it?"

"Understood." Hatch kept her composure as well. "If you don't believe me, make a call to Jimmy's Diner. Ask for Louise. She'll confirm what I've told you."

Santiago paused for a moment before taking a step back and creating some distance between them as she pulled her cellphone from her back pocket. After connecting with the diner and speaking briefly with Louise, she hung up and looked at Hatch.

"You can put your hands down now." Santiago pulled out a notepad and pen. "You said your name is Rachel? Last name, again?"

"Hatch. That's what I prefer to be called."

"You go by your last name?" Santiago raised an eyebrow, looking up at her from the pad of paper in her hand. "You ex-law enforcement or military?"

"Both. Former Military Police."

"Marines?"

"Army."

"Got any ID?" Sweat started to penetrate the underarms of Santiago's shirt.

Hatch produced the military ID card she'd used to force entry into Sophia's apartment. She watched as the detective inspected it, seeming to notice the creases and scratches but offering no comment on her observation. She copied the pertinent information into her notes and handed the ID card back.

A moment of silence hung in the air. Hatch held her breath, waiting for the detective to process the information and make a final determination whether Hatch was one of the good guys or not. The corners of the detective's mouth tightened, and she finally posed a question, her tone edged with both curiosity and annoyance. "Do you always make a point of breaking and entering?"

"I do when I see signs of past forced entry," Hatch replied, her voice steady and unwavering. She jerked her thumb toward the door, drawing attention to the undeniable evidence of a break-in. The pry marks were clear as day, an ominous warning of the danger possibly lurking within.

"Shit," the detective muttered, shaking her head in disbelief. She glanced back at Hatch, her expression a mix of frustration and concession. "Well, that's new."

Hatch met her gaze, her eyes brimming with determination. "It's also a big problem." The unspoken gravity of the situation weighed on them both.

"You find anything inside?"

Hatch considered offering nothing, allowing for the detective to formulate her own opinions. But seeing as how she'd been caught walking out of a missing person's residence after forcing entry, Hatch decided it'd better she if she was as forthcoming as possible.

"Looks like dinner was interrupted, and they left in a hurry. Food still on the table."

"Any signs of struggle?"

"Hard to tell. I'll let you be the judge. Looks like someone's been through here, though. Can't say whether it was done after the fact or not."

Santiago jotted more notes. "I'll take a look."

"You said the pry marks are new?"

"I did," Santiago replied, a touch of hesitancy in her response.

"Do you mind telling me when you last had contact with Sophia?"

"Not sure we're at the stage where I'm answering the questions."

"Humor me. I might prove more valuable than you realize."

"Yesterday." Santiago's voice betrayed her frustration in answering questions from a woman who, only moments ago, was being considered as a suspect in a breaking and entering.

"Sophia's niece said she's been trying to contact her for the past day without luck."

"Could be a lot of reasons for Sophia to make a hasty exit." Santiago looked over her shoulder at the apartment where the shooting took place. "I can think of two just off the top of head."

Hatch gave a slow nod. "I keep going back to these pry marks. Hard to make the argument Sophia made the decision to leave all by herself. Seems to me, she was likely forced."

"I'd be an idiot if I didn't agree on some level with what you're suggesting."

"Any reason you can see for someone wanting to make Sophia disappear?"

"We—well I believe Sophia's a potential witness to the double murder."

"Any suspects?"

"Not yet." There was a subtle hint of frustration in the detective's voice.

"Then there's only a few possibilities I consider to be viable. Either she got scared and took off until things cool down or someone wanted to make sure she didn't speak to law enforcement."

"I'd have to agree."

"Problem is, my gut's telling me it's the latter of the two. And if so, I see only two options. She's either being held against her will or dead. That said, I suggest recovery efforts be a top priority."

"I can assure you they are." Santiago eyed Hatch. "Sounds like you know what you're talking about."

"I've come across similar in my past."

"And based on your experience, what's your gut telling you?"

"I'm one who likes to follow my leads and see where the evidence takes me before I make any conclusions. But I can tell you this, from where I'm standing, things do not look good for Sophia and her children."

Detective Santiago closed her notepad and retrieved a business card from her wallet. She took a moment to write her cell phone number on the back of it before handing it to Hatch. "You find any information on the whereabouts of Miss Sophia and her children, give me a call immediately."

"I will. Feel free to reach out to me should you need anything on my end." Hatch jotted her number along the edge of the card Santiago handed her. She then tore it off and gave it to her.

"Thanks." Santiago gave a questioning look. "I don't typically discuss ongoing investigations with civilians. But tell you what, you find Sophia, and I'll be more open to it."

"Understood. Just putting it out there." Hatch gave a nod. The two exchanged a quick goodbye, and Hatch headed down the stairs. She looked up to see Santiago already hunched near the door, snapping a picture of the marks with her cellphone's camera. Hatch called back up to her, "One more thing, Detective? Do me a favor and find her. It's better if you do."

Santiago looked over her phone and down at Hatch with a questioning look tinged with a hint of annoyance. "And why's that?"

"If things are as bleak as they seem, the cleanup on my end tends to get a bit messy."

"Is that some kind of threat?"

"No. It's just a statement of fact." Hatch shrugged. "You seem like a good cop. Figured I'd give you advance notice."

"By the way, how much is the family paying you to find her?"

"Nothing."

"You're doing this out of the kindness of your own heart?" Santiago's face was etched with confusion and disbelief.

"They seem like good people. In this world, good people are becoming harder to come by. Figured when I come across one in need, I do everything I can to help."

"You're a strange duck, Hatch. But I like the sound of your quack." Santiago offered a half-smile and returned to the task at hand.

Hatch walked back to the PT Cruiser. She sat inside for a moment before pulling away, allowing for the air conditioning to kick in. She looked at the detective's business card and entered the number into her contacts on her cell before tossing it aside and driving away.

As Hatch put Sophia's apartment complex in the rearview, she tapped the screen on her phone and placed a call.

The man answered after the second ring. "Tracy."

Hatch cut right to the chase. "I need you to see if you can track someone down." Hatch gave Tracy the information she had on Sophia, rattling it off before he could argue otherwise. Answering the question before he asked, Hatch said, "She's a potential witness of a double homicide from the night before. The family asked me to look into it."

"You moonlighting as a PI now?" Tracy asked, layering concern into the words.

"Just doing the right thing when opportunity presents."

"Sometimes your need to do the right things has a way of spiraling into chaos."

"Chaos comes with the territory. It's our job to manage it."

"Sounds like there's no convincing you otherwise," Tracy conceded. "I'll see what I can do on my end. I'll be in touch if and when I find anything."

"One more thing." Hatch spoke with a slight hesitancy in her voice, knowing that she'd already pushed the envelope with her de facto boss. "Had a little run in with local law enforcement. Don't think it's an issue. Just want you on notice, should I need you to run some interference on my behalf."

"I've got your back. I hope you know that. But damnit if you don't test my resolve." Tracy sighed. "Let law enforcement do their job."

"As long as they do, I won't have to." Hatch ended the call. Before she could place the phone on the center console, she received an incoming call from an unknown number with a Florida area code. She considered letting it go to voicemail, but curiosity got the best of her and she answered on the third ring.

"Hello. This is Rachel Hatch, correct?" A gruff male voice said from the other end.

"Yes."

"This is First Sergeant Hurley. We met at Gunnery Sergeant Ryker's home earlier."

"Good to hear from you. Anything I can do for you?"

"Wondering if you're still interest in having that talk you asked about."

"Just tell me the where and when, and I'll be there."

# TWENTY-FOUR

HATCH DROVE THE SHORT DISTANCE TO THE BAR HURLEY HAD SUGGESTED. She parked the rental on the adjacent street along the curb. The surrounding shops and restaurants were older but well cared for and had a charm all their own. The night air was not much different in the way of heat and humidity, the only reprieve was the respite from the beating sun. She walked along the sidewalk leading to Skully's Tavern. A sign hung above the main entrance, skull and crossbones etched into the tattered wood.

Hatch walked inside. Music played from an old juke box in the corner. 70s rock resonated across the small dining area. She recognized the tune, but not the song's name or its artist. The music fell into the backdrop as she made her way to the bar where First Sergeant Hurley sat. He was no longer in his formal wear from earlier, exchanging his dress uniform for civilian attire much like Hatch's.

"Almost didn't recognize you," Hatch said as she approached. Of course, that wasn't the case. The career Marine would likely keep groomed high and tight for years beyond his service, as many in his chosen profession often did.

"Rachel, glad you could make it." Hurley gave a tightlipped smile. "Pull up a stool."

"People usually call me Hatch." She slid onto the barstool next to the chiseled Marine and sunk into the worn leather covering as she bellied up to the bar.

"Hatch it is then." Hurley flagged the bartender who made quick work of responding. He cocked his head toward Hatch. "What's your poison?"

She looked at the near empty tumbler of what she assumed was either whiskey or bourbon. "I'll have whatever he's having."

Hurley gave an approving nod. "Make it two bourbons. Three fingers. Neat."

"How's Renee holding up?"

"She's a tough woman." Hurley drained the remnants from his current glass in anticipation of the next and slid it across the lacquered bar in the direction of the man pouring the next round. He let out a long, slow sigh, releasing the burn into the air. "But a loss like that's never easy, regardless."

Hatch knew, all too well, the truth behind those words. "I regret not being able to see Ryker again."

"It's like that sometime, as I'm sure you know. I've lost Marines under my command in the past. Comes with the territory, I guess." The bartender set out the glasses in front of them. Hurley grabbed his and took a pull, knocking a finger off in one gulp. "I remember every single one of them. Never thought I'd be adding another to the roster once I got back stateside."

"About that. Can you tell me about what happened?" Hatch picked up her glass, swirling the amber liquid before taking a sip. The bourbon hit the back of her throat. Heat invaded her chest, the warmth rising to her cheeks and making them redden.

"It's technically still under review by the base investigator." Hurley's face tightened. "Not sure it's something I can go into great detail about at the moment."

"I understand. Not my place." Hatch set her glass down. "I'm not in the game anymore. Civilian status doesn't hold much clout. I get that. I guess I was just hoping for an idea of what happened. Not the details."

Hurley grunted. He took another pull from his glass, this time sipping rather than gulping. "I can say this. It was an accident. A terrible one. But an accident nonetheless."

Hatch nodded but remained quiet, allowing the power of silence to apply the right amount of pressure. It was a trick she'd learned long ago. Silence was one of the secrets to an effective interrogation. Too often, the discomfort that came with it led investigators to fill in the noise with comments or questions of their own, diminishing the likelihood of extracting a confession.

"You get that in the service?" Hurley gestured toward Hatch's scar.

"I did."

"Then you've been in the shit?"

Hatch gave a slow nod. "Sometimes I feel like I'm still in it. Or at least covered in its unmistakable stink."

"Then you get it. You understand that bad things happen." Hurley shook his head. "Some things are just out of our control."

"I take it you're saying this was one of those times?"

Hurley stared at the half-empty glass in front of him as if the answer was hidden somewhere at the bottom. "You ever replay an event over and over again in your mind, hoping the outcome changes?"

"Definition of insanity. And the answer's yes." Hatch thought of Cruise. She'd gone back in time a thousand times since.

"He fell from the chopper during a demo." Hurley's shoulders slumped. "He fell, and I couldn't save him."

"Some things are out of our control, out of our grasp." Hatch looked into the pained eyes of her bar mate. "I don't know you personally. But I know the type. And understanding what I do about soldiers like you means if you couldn't have saved Ryker, then it's doubtful anyone could've."

Hurley downed the rest of his bourbon and raised his empty glass for the bartender. After seeing his unspoken order had been received, he set it down on the bar and rubbed his hands over his face. "That means a lot. Thank you."

Hatch sipped at her drink, bringing the level of amber to the halfway point, in no way matching the pace of her counterpart. An even tempo meant an even mind for Hatch. It had been a long time since she'd overindulged and, under the emotional volatility of the moment, she chose to keep it that way.

"Tell me a little bit about yourself. A friend of Ryker's is a friend of mine. And I like to know the company I keep."

His words and tone were friendly enough, but the years of commanding troops made everything he said sound like an order. Being the good soldier she was, Hatch obeyed. "Not much to tell. Did fifteen in the Army. Got banged up, and they told me to pack my bags."

"Is that the mark of that day?" He nodded to her scarred arm. "The one that cut your career short?"

"It is. At least it's the one you can see. The real mark is on the inside. I've spent every day since trying to find a way to heal it."

"Any luck? I could sure use a bit of it right now."

"Not sure I'm the Dear Abby advice giver you seek." Hatch made a weak attempt at a smile. "Some days are better than others. As far as coping goes, I try to honor the lives lost by putting my skills to work helping others in need."

"Like a guardian angel?"

"Never thought of it that way before. It comes from my father. He had bestowed his code on me." Hatch swirled her glass, watching the amber vortex form within. "Help good people and punish those who do them harm."

"Sounds like I would've liked your father. I assume he was military, too."

"Snake eater."

"Special Forces. I spent a good portion of my time with First Recon." Hurley suddenly had a faraway look in his eyes. The nostalgia playing through his mind went beyond the wall of liquor bottles lining the mirror-backed shelf he was staring at. "Best years of my life were spent there."

"Mine too."

Hurley broke from his trance and turned toward Hatch. "You were SF?"

Hatch had gotten this response on numerous occasions and wasn't offended by the question or the expression on the gruff First Sergeant's face. "Yes."

"I'll be damned." Hurley's head bobbed. A look of respect replaced the questioning one he'd given upon first hearing her claim. "That must be a hell of a story."

Hatch shrugged. "Everyone's got one. Mine's nothing special."

"I beg to differ. You've got to be the first female I've met to make it through the qual course."

"First to make it through twice."

"Well, that's one I've got to hear." The bartender replaced Hurley's empty for a fresh one, but the Marine remained fixated on Hatch. "Do tell."

"Maybe another time." Hatch drained the rest of her bourbon, the liquid's burn more muted now. "I've got an early rise tomorrow."

"Heading home? I know it'd mean a lot to Renee if you were able to attend the funeral."

"We'll see. Not a big fan of hospitals and graveyards." Hatch wanted to add oceans and lakes to the list but felt it would force an explanation, one she wasn't prepared to give, wondering if she ever would.

"I get it. Just think about it." Hurley had slowed his pace with the booze in his hand. "So, what's got you chasing the sunrise?"

"Helping someone find a missing family member."

"Does this have to do with that code of yours?"

Hatch nodded. "I don't look for it, but somehow it seems to find me, nonetheless."

"Maybe you're a beacon. For those in a dark place, you provide light."

"Never thought about it that way before. I always thought of myself as more of a shit magnet."

Hurley erupted with a laugh, slapping the bar with the palm of his hand. "Keep fighting the good fight. And if there's anything you ever need on my end, don't hesitate. When the shit starts flying, I'm a pretty good wingman to have at your side."

"I believe you on that. And thank you. For both the drink and the conversation." Hatch pushed back from the bar and stood. "If we don't cross paths again before I head off, I just wanted to say that it's been an honor to meet you. Ryker was lucky to have served under your command."

Hurley stood. He was four inches taller, but in that moment, the two stood as equals. A hearty handshake was exchanged, and they parted ways and Hatch headed for the door.

She looked back in the direction of Hurley, who had already turned and was addressing the bourbon in his hand, before stepping out into the muggy air.

She made her way back to the rental car. With closure given to Ryker's death, Hatch focused her mind on finding Sophia. The quicker, the better. She was looking to put some distance between herself and the sadness of Panama City.

Just as she put the PT Cruiser into drive, her cellphone buzzed. Hatch looked down at the caller ID. She didn't recognize the number, except that she noted the area code was local. She picked up on the third ring. "Hatch."

"Hi—um—Rachel? It's Renee."

"Hi. I didn't recognize the number." Hatch heard a sniffle and the thick sadness in her voice. "Everything okay?"

"No."

Hatch didn't speak. She gave Renee the time to formulate whatever had motivated the call.

"Can we talk?"

"Of course. I'm here to listen."

"Not over the phone."

"Sure thing. Name the time and place." Hatch's interest was piqued. "I can meet you now, if you'd like?"

"Tomorrow morning would be better. I just got Amanda to sleep. It's been a rough time."

"No need to explain. Tomorrow it is. Got somewhere in mind?"

"I can drop Amanda with my mom in the morning. You can come by here whenever you're able."

"Sounds perfect." Hatch let the conversation pause for a moment. "Is this about Jeff?"

"Yes. There's more to the story. I'm probably overthinking things but —" Renee's voice trailed off.

"Sometimes it helps to talk. Works to clear the mind."

"Tomorrow will be a good thing, then. I've got a lot of clearing to do."

Hatch set a time to meet with Renee before ending the call. She sat for a moment, her foot on the brake, giving time for the rental's air conditioning to work its magic. Hatch thought of the distress she'd heard in Renee's voice. She wondered if it was just the burden of grief building up, the recently widowed wife of her friend looking for comfort outside her circle. Probably.

Then again, Hatch was a self-proclaimed shit magnet, and she started considering the possibility of the impending storm that usually accompanied a phone call like that. She hoped she was wrong. She hoped not to turn Tracy's warning into a reality. But hope was for dreamers. And Hatch didn't live in the clouds. Her world was grounded in the truth forged by experience.

As she pulled out from her spot, she knew one thing was certain: tomorrow's conversation with Renee would determine if the track record of her past would continue into the present.

# TWENTY-FIVE

HATCH ARRIVED AT THE RYKER HOUSE. NO MARINES LINED THE WALK. THE quiet stillness that followed the initial outpouring of support after a death often dropped off rapidly as the rest of the world continued to spin, leaving the bereaved to mourn. Hatch sat on the couch where First Sergeant Hurley had sat the other morning. The somberness continued, but Renee had already begun taking the first steps toward finding her footing in this new phase of her life.

"You said you had something to tell me?" Hatch asked, her voice a blend of compassion and curiosity.

Renee tugged at the edges of her sleeves as she began to confide in Hatch. "There was always money, you know? Appearing out of nowhere, and always cash. He'd come up with some weak excuse, but I never pushed him too hard for an explanation."

Hatch studied Renee's face, her eyes reflecting the weight of her guilt. "Why didn't you ask him more about it?" Hatch asked gently.

Renee sighed, looking down at her hands. "Truth is, I didn't want to know. I suspected it was from something illegal, but..." She hesitated, her voice cracking. "For once, we had enough money to take care of things around the house, to give our daughter a better life. I even managed to get her into a good private school. It was as if those crisp bills were a lifeline, and I was too afraid to let go."

Hatch nodded, understanding the pull of that lifeline. "What else can you tell me?"

Renee's voice grew quieter. "Ryker's hours were always strange. He'd say he was off for a late night with the boys, but over time, I started to notice something." She paused. Her brow furrowed. "On those nights, the local news would report a string of robberies. It was like clockwork."

Hatch's expression turned serious. "You think Ryker and his friends were involved?"

Renee shook her head, her eyes welling with tears. "I don't know. I just can't shake the feeling that it's more than a coincidence."

Hatch reached out and placed a reassuring hand on Renee's arm. "Don't worry, we'll get to the bottom of this. You did the right thing by telling me."

Renee nodded, giving a weak smile, and opened her laptop on the coffee table in front of them. When she brought up the browser, the screen illuminated with a history of old news reports. The couch creaked beneath her as she leaned in, clicking through each article. Hatch watched as Renee's shoulders slumped further with each article she presented. There was no more denying the obvious connection. The evidence was mounting, and Hatch saw that Renee could no longer deny the truth.

Hatch put a comforting arm around Renee's shoulder, reassuring her as she scrolled through with tear-filled eyes. She stopped on the most recent article. The double homicide. The woman nearly doubled over, her features riddled with disappointment, anger, and sorrow.

"Was the money in the duffle bag part of all this?" Hatch asked, her voice low and soft. "Do you think Hurley was trying to buy your silence?"

Renee choked back a sob and shrugged, wiping away the tears that streaked her cheeks. "I'd like to think it was out of the kindness of his heart. He said the guys pooled the money to help me out. Those guys were like brothers to Ryker, and Hurley...Hurley was like a father in a lot of ways."

Hatch sat down across from Renee, her gaze steady and understanding. "I know this is hard. But the police need to know the truth. You're scared. I get that. But we can figure this out together. I'll help get you through this."

Renee's hands covered her mouth and trembled as she sat staring at the article. "I know it's the right thing to do, but the thought of betraying Jeff, of putting my daughter's already-fragile world in jeopardy…I'm just not sure I can do it.

Hatch leaned in, her expression sympathetic yet determined. "Show me the dates, Renee. Let's see if there's a pattern. Let me look at it objectively before we jump to any conclusions."

With a shaky breath, Renee opened her planner, revealing the scribbled notes that tracked her husband's late-night excursions. Hatch examined the entries, her eyes flicking between the dates and the list of robbery incidents she had compiled.

"Interesting," Hatch murmured, jotting down the correlating dates in her own notebook. "There's a definite pattern here. Whether it's connected beyond coincidence will require some digging."

Renee bit her lip, tears threatening to spill from her eyes. "What do I do now, Hatch? I'm so scared."

"I recently spoke to a detective who's looking into these robberies," Hatch said. "I think it's important you talk to her. It'll be better coming from you."

Renee's eyes widened, fear consuming her. "But what if Hurley finds out? What if his men come after me or my daughter?"

"They'd have to get through me to do that." Hatch softened her gaze. "It's a lot harder a thing than some realize. Some have had to learn that lesson the hard way."

Hatch smiled, knowing she had helped Renee make the right choice. They both understood the risks, but sometimes doing the right thing meant facing the storm head-on.

Hatch stood and handed Detective Santiago's business card to Renee, her eyes locking with the younger woman's for a moment. "You'll want to call her," she said quietly. "She'll help."

Renee took the card with trembling fingers, her eyes welling up with unshed tears. "Thank you, Hatch. For everything."

A heavy silence settled between them. The bond forged during their short time together was now a palpable force. Hatch's heart ached, knowing she was leaving a part of herself behind with Renee. "Take care of yourself, Renee. I know you'll find your way."

Renee nodded, wiping away a tear that escaped down her cheek. "What about you? What are you going to do now?"

Hatch's jaw set, determination blazing in her eyes. "I have some other business to attend to."

The moment lingered, Hatch's promise hanging heavy in the air. She turned, stepping off the porch, her stride purposeful and strong. As she slid behind the wheel of her car, she glanced at the rearview mirror, watching Renee clutch the business card as if it were a lifeline.

Hatch pulled out her phone and dialed Santiago's number, hearing the line ring before it went to voicemail. "Santiago, it's Hatch. Expect a call from Renee Ryker. I'll reconnect with you later." She ended the call, her voice clipped and concise.

With her mission clear, Hatch set her sights on the next step: contacting the NCIS agent handling the investigation into Ryker's death.

# TWENTY-SIX

SANTIAGO LEANED BACK IN HER WORN OFFICE CHAIR, THE FAINT AROMA OF stale coffee and musty papers filling the air. Panama City Police Department's investigation unit was not a luxurious place, but it was where she felt most alive—where she belonged. Her thoughts drifted back to the scene at the stairwell, the blood she'd recovered. Still no word from Orson had her beginning to wonder if he'd hold up his end of the bargain.

Her eyes darted between her notes and the screen, her fingers typing rapidly as she recounted the information she had gleaned. The two patrolmen, Baxter and Green, had been ruled out for the footprints found in the blood. She uploaded the photos and comparisons she'd taken outside of the roll call room.

The reality of Sophia White and her children now missing had sunk in. Santiago couldn't shake the image of the pry marks, an ominous sign of foul play. Her conscience screamed at her to act, to find the woman and her children before it was too late.

Santiago thought of the encounter with Hatch, the mysterious woman working on behalf of Sophia's niece. Santiago had confirmed her story with a call to the diner, but she didn't include any of that in the report. It was an instinct, a gut feeling that Hatch could somehow help her piece together this dark puzzle. She hoped she was right.

Her patience was running thin as she waited for Detective Malcolm to appear. But the ticking clock on the wall reminded her that time was slipping away. With every passing second, the danger to Sophia White and her children increased. Santiago took a deep breath, and pulled her shoulders back, attempting to alleviate some of the built-up tension.

Her finger hovered over the submit button, ready to unleash a chain of events that could either help solve the case or bring down her career. She glanced at Captain Parnell as he sifted through a stack of papers. She knew the consequences, but she couldn't stand by any longer. With a slow exhale, she pressed the button, sealing her fate.

As the report was sent for review, Santiago peeked around the corner of her cubicle partition, watching as Captain Parnell shifted his attention to the computer monitor. She felt her heart race, the adrenaline coursing through her veins like a torrential river. There was no turning back now. All she could do was hope her actions would ultimately save lives, even if it meant risking her own career in the process.

Just then, Detective Malcolm burst into the room, his footsteps echoing across the office. Santiago could feel his stare, and as she swiveled in her chair to face him, she braced herself for the inevitable confrontation. With fury etched into every line of his face, Malcolm stalked toward her, his gait filled with purpose.

Santiago squared her shoulders as Malcolm towered over her desk, his voice booming through the office space. "What the hell do you think you're doing?"

Unruffled, Santiago folded her arms and met his gaze. "You'll have to be more specific, Detective. I'm not familiar with your brand of subtlety."

The restrained tone of her response only served to stoke the fire of Malcolm's anger. For a moment, Santiago thought he might come undone. "You had no right to submit that blood evidence without my knowledge!" he spat, his face reddening with each word.

With a dismissive flick of her wrist, Santiago retorted, "Maybe if you did your job properly, I wouldn't have to step in."

Malcolm's eyes flashed with rage, but as he opened his mouth to speak, no words came out. Instead, he spun on his heel and charged toward Captain Parnell's office, slamming the door shut behind him. Even through the barrier, Santiago could hear the muffled sound of Malcolm's tirade.

Parnell looked past Malcolm and through the window of his office, his gaze settling on Santiago. She could see the conflict in his eyes—anger mixed with a deep, unspoken sadness. The knot in her stomach tightened, a sense of foreboding settling in.

Malcolm finally emerged from the office, leaving the door wide open as he stormed back to his desk. As he passed Santiago, he made a point to lock eyes with her. She knew things had taken a turn for the worse when he offered a cocky smile before sitting down.

Captain Parnell said nothing, just motioned with one finger. Santiago felt the gazes of each of her peers upon her as she made her way to his office, answering his silent request. Unlike Malcolm, she didn't slam the door. She could feel the impending doom and took each stride carefully. She sat in front of Parnell. He still had the same conflicted look on his face. He rubbed his cheeks with his hands, leaving them a blotchy red.

Santiago had faced a lot of critical incidents in her time as a cop, more than most. Even so, she felt a pang of anxiety encroaching from her extremities and constricting her heart. She tried to breathe deep to combat the constriction, but the shallow breaths wouldn't relent.

Parnell spoke, his words coming to her as if they were having an underwater tea party. "I gave you a strict warning. This didn't come from me. It came from above. But you already knew that. Mind telling me if you remember what I said?"

Santiago had no witty reply. She offered a sheepish shrug and said, "Not to interfere with Malcolm's case."

Parnell pursed his lips. "I don't know how I could've made that any clearer. I'm also left with no choice."

Parnell seemed saddened by his own words. This only worsened the sickening feeling she had.

"Captain, did you get a chance to read my report? Did you see the findings? I mean, c'mon, Malcolm missed blood evidence. Resisted any notion of it—"

Parnell cut her off with a sweep of his hand. "Doesn't matter. You've stepped outside your investigative responsibilities after being specifically told not to. My hands are tied on this one."

Santiago's fire returned, the case and its potential implications superseding the fear she felt. "Not only did Malcolm completely ignore the possibility of additional evidence, but he's also turned a blind eye to a potential witness, who, by the way, is now missing."

Parnell's shoulders dipped, and his voice lowered as he spoke. "I'm not saying what you've presented doesn't have its own merit, but you went about it the wrong way. You overstepped yourself. And the warning I gave you... You've now forced my hand. I have no other choice but to put you on a leave of absence, effective immediately."

Santiago knew Parnell had been leading to this. But it didn't lessen the blow once delivered. She sank in her chair. They say that when facing death, people see their life flash before their eyes. Santiago believed it to be true. Sitting in her captain's office, she felt the impending death of a career she'd spent the better part of her adult life building. She thought of all the sacrifices. She wondered if everything she'd worked for had been for naught.

She looked at her captain, figuring if she was going down, she'd go down fighting. "You need to look at this objectively," Santiago said. "Those boot prints I found in the blood evidence I submitted were tactical treads. You've got a detective assigned to the case who is unwilling to put forth any investigative effort to resolve those issues."

Parnell looked like he was going to interrupt, but Santiago continued, "You've also got a key witness who's now missing. I documented my findings when I went back to her apartment. There's evidence of foul play. If she and her children aren't dead yet, they're running on borrowed time."

Parnell's eyes flicked to Santiago, dark and intense, as he held up his hand, halting her. "I hear you, Santiago. I've read your report, and I believe there are things that need to be followed up on. As for Sophia and her children, I've already told Malcolm to work up an alert so we can locate her."

Santiago's worry dissipated, but not entirely. She leaned forward, casting a glance back at Malcolm, who stood with his back to her. In a low whisper, she said, "Ever think about why a detective would turn down the possibility of pertinent evidence and information related to a major case? Ever put any thought into the fact that this robbery crew has managed to duck law enforcement for months without a trace? And here I am, presenting tangible evidence capable of blowing this thing wide open, and the detective in charge of the investigation disregards all of it." A loud groan erupted from Santiago at the mounting stress. "I mean, I get it. Malcolm and I are oil and vinegar. No doubt about it. I'd be hard-pressed to piss on him if he were on fire, but when it comes to a case, all that crap gets shoved aside. Especially when you've got a double murder. But not Malcolm. He's either the laziest, most incompetent detective this side of the Mississippi or—"

Santiago paused, watching Parnell's expression shift as he said, "Watch what you say next. Because if it's what I think, you better be prepared to face the fallout."

Santiago leveled a gaze at her supervisor, the steely conviction returning as she continued. "I think you've got a dirty cop in play here. And my bet's on Malcolm. I'm willing to accept if I'm wrong. Hell, I'm already suspended for trying to help. Just promise me this—you'll take a hard look at the evidence. And take a harder look at Malcolm."

Parnell gave a slow nod. He then eyed the badge on her hip and swallowed hard. Santiago knew the drill. She unclipped her badge and slid it across the table, knocking a file folder to the edge of the desk. She then unholstered her duty weapon, taking a moment to clear it, and set the empty Glock with its slide locked back and the magazine alongside her badge.

Parnell unlocked a drawer and placed the items inside before closing and locking it. He gave a weak attempt at a smile and said, "You're still a good cop. None of this changes that."

Santiago rolled her eyes as she pushed back in her seat and stood. "Doesn't look that way from where I stand." She turned to walk out and stopped. Without looking back, she said, "Find Sophia and her kids. I'd hate for there to be more bodies, especially innocent ones, added to this shitshow."

Parnell cleared his throat and said, "You have my word."

Santiago said nothing else before exiting, leaving Parnell to weigh the heavy accusations and consequences of his decisions.

Santiago strode purposefully to her desk, her face a mask of steely determination. She gathered her belongings, her hands shaking as she snatched them all up. Instinctively, her fingers sought the keys to her department-issued sedan, a privilege she'd taken for granted as a detective. Now, with her status as a detective hanging in the balance, the ride was no longer hers to claim.

With her jaw clenched and her eyes fixed on some distant point, Santiago navigated the maze of cubicles and offices with a determined stride. It took all her strength to resist the urge to march over to Malcolm's desk and bury her fist into his smug, unsuspecting face. She couldn't risk it, not when her career dangled by a single, fraying thread.

Emerging from the precinct into the blinding sunlight, Santiago's mind raced with a fervor that matched the blazing orb above. She fumbled in her pocket for her phone, her heart pounding in her chest as she prepared to take the final, humbling step. With a trembling hand, she dialed the number.

The familiar, soothing tones of her mother's voice washed over her like a tide, and Santiago nearly choked on the words she had to force out. Her voice wavered, barely a whisper, as she asked for the one thing she'd sworn never to need again: a ride home.

The line went silent for a beat, and then her mother's voice, filled with concern and understanding, agreed to come to her rescue. As Santiago hung up the phone, she swallowed the bitter taste of her own pride, and her resolve hardened like tempered steel.

# TWENTY-SEVEN

CAIN'S BOOTS CRUNCHED ON THE GRAVEL AS HE APPROACHED THE FAMILIAR rendezvous point, the abandoned warehouse looming like a specter on the outskirts of Panama City, Florida. The sun was dipping toward the horizon, casting long shadows across the desolate landscape, but the heat remained suffocating. He eyed Gypsy, with his wild hair and untamed beard, standing in the same spot as before, waiting.

"You sure about Hatch?" Gypsy asked, his voice gravelly as Cain neared. The skepticism in his tone was as thick as the humidity in the air.

"Positive," Cain replied, wiping sweat from his brow. "She bought the accident story. She'll be out of our hair soon enough."

Gypsy squinted at Cain, his eyes narrowing into slits. "I don't like taking chances," he growled. "Maybe we should call off the next job."

Cain's heart quickened, his mind racing at the thought of losing the largest payday of his life. He needed to convince Gypsy that Rachel Hatch was no threat.

"Look," Cain said, his voice steady and confident, "she was just curious about Ryker's call. That's all. Trust me." He flashed an arrogant smile. "I can be very persuasive when I need to be. I don't think she suspects a thing. Besides, we don't need any more bodies. We've got enough heat on us as it is."

Gypsy's eyes never left Cain's. He flicked the dying embers of his cigarette to the ground and lit another, continuing his perpetual chain-smoking. Inhaling deeply, Gypsy exhaled a cloud of smoke and shifted the conversation.

"What about Sophia?" he asked, the smoke wreathing his face. "You found her yet? The mother of two who saw you that night?"

Cain's jaw tightened at a reminder of what started this downward spiral. "Swift's on it. So far, she's a ghost. But we're not giving up."

"If she shows her face, she's our top priority. You understand?" Gypsy's eyes bore into Cain.

Cain nodded, his expression solemn. "I understand."

Gypsy seemed to accept Cain's assurance, but the warning in his voice was unmistakable. "I'll take Hatch off the list for now. But if she starts sniffing around, you know what needs to be done."

Cain's gut twisted, but his face remained impassive. He nodded again, the weight of Gypsy's words settling in. Whatever it took to survive, he would do what had to be done.

The air between them crackled with anticipation as he exchanged terse words with Gypsy. "We're on for tomorrow night, right?" he asked, his voice barely above a whisper.

Gypsy nodded, eyes narrowing in focus. "Good to go. I'll iron out the details and brief the team later."

The two men parted ways, the tension between them dissipating as they went their separate paths. Cain slid into his car, the engine roaring to life as he hit the gas. In the rearview mirror, Gypsy's figure became smaller and smaller, swallowed by the distance. Just as Cain began to lose himself in thoughts of the upcoming operation, his phone buzzed to life.

"We've got a problem," Swift's voice crackled through the speaker, and Cain couldn't help but let out an exasperated sigh. "What now?"

"The Hatch woman just paid Renee a visit," Swift replied. Cain could hear the urgency in his tone. The news sent a shiver down his spine, igniting a fire within him that threatened to consume his composure.

Swift hesitated before continuing, and Cain's blood began to boil. "The bug you planted the other morning picked up most of it. Hatch planted the seed. Renee did some digging. She pieced it all together."

Cursing under his breath, Cain reached for the whiskey flask in the console, his knuckles white. He unscrewed the cap and downed the remainder in one swift motion, the burn of the alcohol doing nothing to quench the inferno within him, instead adding to it.

"Anything else?" he spat, his voice strained and impatient.

Swift cleared his throat. "Hatch convinced her to speak to the cops. She gave her a card for a Detective Santiago."

The news hit Cain like a sucker punch, leaving him gasping for air. As his vision swam, the road ahead of him blurred into a whirlwind of uncertainty. The operation that had seemed so close to fruition was suddenly on the brink of crumbling, all because of one woman. Rachel Hatch.

And Cain knew, with a chilling certainty, that he would do whatever it took to silence her.

The sun dipped below the horizon, its dying rays painting the sky in shades of orange and red, a beautiful, almost apocalyptic sight. He could feel the heaviness in his chest; things having been set in motion that now seemed beyond his control. But there was no turning back, not when the stakes were this high.

He glanced at the metal flask on the floorboard, its contents now irrelevant. The drink that had once been a source of solace now felt like a bitter reminder of the choices he had made. The road ahead seemed to stretch into infinity, and he knew that it was a path he could not turn away from.

As the darkness crept in, swallowing the last traces of daylight, Cain's thoughts were consumed by the tangled web of consequences that lay ahead. Renee's loyalty had always been a point of pride for him, but now, he found himself questioning the very foundations of their bond. He knew she was in danger, and it tore at him to think that he might be the one to put her in harm's way.

The hum of the engine filled the silence as he drove, his mind racing faster than the miles passing beneath his wheels. The inevitable confrontation with Hatch loomed large in his thoughts, a specter that haunted him. He knew that if he couldn't find a way to contain the situation, the consequences would be catastrophic.

As the first stars began to emerge in the night sky, Cain felt a chill that had nothing to do with the cooling air outside. He knew that Gypsy would make good on his promise to deal with the cop, Santiago. That knowledge did little to ease his conscience. He had wanted power and control, and now he found himself caught in a web of his own making, struggling to hold on to the very things he thought he'd gained.

Cain's jaw clenched as he forced his focus back to the task at hand. He knew that tomorrow's business had to come first, that he needed to keep his priorities straight. But as he drove on into the night, the faces of Renee and Hatch, their lives now compromised by their exposure to the truth, refused to leave him. He knew that he would have to face them soon enough, and he prayed that he would find the strength to do what needed to be done.

For deep down, in the darkest corners of his soul, Cain understood that there was no turning back, not anymore. The die had been cast, the path chosen, and now all he could do was face the consequences, whatever they might be.

# TWENTY-EIGHT

Tracy had come through for her. He'd located Sophia, using some next gen facial recognition software, at a gas station. From there, he'd been able to pinpoint her location, confirming it with the motel manager when he called posing to be a state police officer looking for a vehicle involved in a hit-and-run crash. It had taken some effort on Tracy's part, and Hatch knew she was on the hook to pay back the debt.

Hatch followed her GPS outside the city limits to the motel in the middle of nowhere. A smart place to run away to. The fact that Tracy had to go the long route to track Sophia down meant that she'd likely used cash, since credit card transactions would have expedited the effort.

She parked in a dark corner of the lot. Armed with the room number, Hatch sat in her rental car and watched the strip of motel rooms. The setup was much like Oak's motel where Hatch was staying but didn't appear to have the charm added by the dedicated owner.

Hatch watched a drunk male stagger out of a pickup. A woman, dressed in a leather skirt and halter top, popped out of the passenger side. She navigated the gravel lot in heels, exacerbating the appearance of her intoxication. They made their way to room number three. Sophia was staying with her children in room number four.

The slurred voices dissipated in volume as they entered their room and closed the door. Hatch remained in her vehicle under the cover of darkness for a few more minutes, ensuring the coast was clear. Satisfied it was, she exited and made her way over to the door.

Hatch heard the soft murmurs of a woman followed by the giggles of young children. Her heart lifted at the knowledge that Sophia had escaped those looking to silence her, at least for the moment.

Hatch knocked on the door, delivering three controlled raps. The happy chatter inside hushed. The female voice spoke in a low whisper, indecipherable through the door. Shuffling feet indicated someone had approached the door. Hatch heard a gentle brushing against the door and figured Sophia was looking through the peephole to see who was there.

"We're not taking solicitors," the woman behind the door said.

"I'm not soliciting," Hatch replied. "I'm here on behalf of your niece, Louise?"

After a beat of silence, a lock on the door unlatched, and the knob made a noise from the inside. The door opened as far as the safety chain would allow, revealing a woman around Hatch's age, maybe a little younger. She looked at Hatch with tired eyes, now filled with concern and confusion.

"You said my niece sent you?" Sophia asked. "She doesn't even know I'm here. She's not supposed to, anyway." The woman looked Hatch up and down with wide eyes, then a look over her shoulder as if checking on her kids in an entirely different room. "Look, I don't want any trouble—"

"I'm here to help." Hatch put her hands up in a gesture of surrender. "You're not in trouble with me, but I know you're in trouble. And handling it is kind of my forte."

Sophia's breathing quickened, and she placed a hand on her chest as though trying to calm herself down by just the warmth of her palm.

"I know this is a lot to take in, but I'm going to need you to trust me."

"Is this about the other night?" Sophia asked, her tone defensive and her voice raised. Her arms were folded now. Her response was driven by fear. Her raised voice wobbled when she spoke again. "Are you a detective? Because I already told them I didn't see anything."

"I'm no detective. And the people who are looking for you don't care that you won't talk. That's never going to be enough of a guarantee."

Hatch saw the fear in Sophia's eyes. "I'm assuming you already know that. Otherwise, you wouldn't have taken all these precautions to stay off the radar."

"But you were able to find me." Sophia looked back at her children, whose heads were peeking out from the bathroom.

"I've got resources at my disposal others don't. But that's neither here nor there. The fact that I did find you, means there's a possibility the others will too."

"Then you know who they are?"

"I've got a pretty good theory. Still gathering the proof." Hatch continued to scan the parking lot as headlights swept over them, announcing the arrival of another vehicle. "I think it's best if we talk inside. Do you mind?"

Sophia hesitated for only a moment before releasing the chain and stepping aside so Hatch could enter. She closed and locked the door behind her.

"Try to stay calm," Hatch said, her own voice almost a whisper. "I believe the people you saw the other night are a group of highly trained Marines."

"Why would military men be going after drug dealers?"

"The same reason anyone who enters into a life of crime does. Money."

"I don't understand."

"These guys have been doing this for almost a year. Robbing drug dealers gives them the perfect victim. They deal in cash. Hard to trace. Drug dealers don't like the cops, and vice versa, making for limited probability of capture. But then things went wrong."

"The murders."

"It drew some heat. The fact you were identified as a potential witness, warranted or not, puts you in their crosshairs."

"I just want all of this to end." Sophia fought back tears.

"I'd like to help in that regard. But to do that, I need you to level with me and tell me what you saw."

"Sounds like you've already figured everything out."

"I've got a pretty good idea, but you might know more."

"I thought they were police."

"Why's that?"

"Because they were in all black. Done up with those black ski masks. We see the SWAT people in our complex more than I'd like. I'm pretty familiar."

"Never considered that."

"What?"

"The cop angle." Hatch thought for a moment, contemplating that possibility. Just because she couldn't see the connection to Hurley, didn't mean it didn't exist. "Is there anything else you can tell me?"

"One of the men came back."

"That night?"

Sophia shook her head. "No. The next. I'd seen him. Well, I saw his eyes through the mask. But I recognized him when he came to my door."

"Can you describe him?"

Sophia spent the next minute or so painting a clear picture of the man she saw. Hatch listened intently. And she knew exactly who that man was. Jeff Ryker.

"Not sure anything I told you is beneficial."

"It is. Trust me. The devil's in the details." Hatch tried to give a reassuring smile. "What did the man do when he came to see you?"

"He told me to get out of town. To disappear. Didn't tell me how long, but promised to find me when it was over." Sophia then looked over at a black duffle bag in the corner of the room. "He gave me that. Ten thousand dollars cash."

"Why'd he do that?"

"Told me it would help me lay low. He gave me specific instructions about only using cash."

"Smart. It probably saved your life."

"If you have a way of contacting that man, I'd like you to thank him for me."

"I wish I could, but he's dead." Hatch delivered it with a numbness.

Sophia covered her mouth. "That's terrible. Is it because of me?"

"No. It's because of him. And the decisions he and the others made." Hatch paused, reflecting on the faces of the many enemies she had confronted in her past. "Every choice has a consequence. Some just come with a higher price tag."

"So, what am I supposed to do now?" Desperation seeped from her as she spoke.

"Stay here. Continue to lay low." Hatch saw the fear in her eyes. "I'll be doing my best to assist in bringing these men to justice."

"What if you don't?"

"I don't choose failure as an option. Not in my DNA." Hatch watched as Sophia's eyes ran the length of her scar.

"You've been in this kind of situation before?"

"Every situation is different. But the short answer is yes."

Sophia looked at her boys, then back at Hatch. She gave a slow nod. "I'll do what you say."

"When this is over, you may need to give your statement about what you witnessed. These men don't deserve to see the light of day." Hatch took a step toward the door. "When the time is right, I'll connect you with Detective Santiago. She's working the case."

"I have her card. She stopped by to talk to me."

"Keep that card handy, but don't make any calls. Not until this thing gets sorted out. Understood?"

Sophia nodded. Her youngest son broke from his hiding place and ran to his mother's side. He hugged himself tight against her hips. Sophia put her arm around her son but kept her gaze on Hatch. "This has been rough for them."

Hatch looked at the boys and thought of Jake, and the bravery her nephew had shown. She saw that same spark in Sophia's children. "I won't be back here until this is over. If anyone but me or Detective Santiago show up, do not open this door. You call the police immediately. You're outside city limits, so you'll likely get a trooper or sheriff's deputy."

"So, we just wait?"

"Afraid so." Hatch tried to ease the mother's worry but knew there was likely little she could say that would. "You seem like a good mother, a good person. I'll do everything in my power to keep you safe."

Hatch looked out the peephole before stepping out. Noise from the neighboring drunkards accompanied her on the walk back to the PT

Cruiser. She watched as Sophia continued to peek through the door before closing it.

Hatch's mind was at peace, knowing that Sophia and her children were safe, at least for the moment, as she drove back toward the city. It was late. She needed to rest. Tomorrow she'd work to find the evidence needed to bring down those responsible.

# TWENTY-NINE

Cain settled into his customary chair, his eyes locked on the large TV screen that displayed the projected surveillance footage. The room was dimly lit, providing an atmosphere of focus and anticipation. As he rubbed his chin thoughtfully, Cain took a sip from his glass, the ice cubes clinking together as his mind raced to formulate the most effective plan of action.

Swift, the tech-savvy member of the group, had managed to procure the footage, transferring it to his computer and then connecting it to the screen for a more comprehensive view. The microdrone he'd used earlier in the day to stealthily capture the images populated the screen. The team watched the footage with rapt attention, each holding a cold beer, taking occasional sips as they pondered the various possibilities and angles.

The building in question appeared abandoned, a relic of a bygone era. Its surroundings were equally desolate, the crumbling infrastructure hinting at a long-forgotten purpose. Encircled by roads on all sides, a small gravel parking lot at the front boasted a smattering of vehicles. It was isolated enough that their entry and exit plan should work to allow them to move without notice. Cain reflected on that. He'd been just as confident the other night at the apartment, and the unimaginable fallout still lingered. He no longer took anything for granted.

Swift paused the video, pulling up a program that transformed the top-down view of the building into a detailed map. With a few clicks, he highlighted the entry and exit points using bright red digital markers, ensuring they were easily identifiable.

Resuming the footage, the drone descended, now capturing an eye-level perspective of the building as it circled its perimeter in a swift, fluid motion. Swift manipulated the speed, slowing the video down to allow the team to carefully observe the various entry and exit points, as well as potential obstacles like windows and other barriers that could impede their access.

As the drone panned to the right of the building, it revealed a garage, its wide doors open to display men smoking cigarettes and tinkering with cars—a hazardous mix, to say the least. Continuing around the right side, a metal fence enclosed the side yard, and a small door connected the yard to the garage. Next to the door, an electrical box beckoned with potential opportunities.

The rear of the building featured a sliding glass door, a possible escape route if things went awry. Windows adorned all four sides of the structure, though they were sparse in number. As the footage played, the team continued to scrutinize every aspect, mentally preparing for the mission ahead and anticipating the challenges they would face.

Cain surveyed the scene before him and declared, "Our most viable point of entry appears to be the front." He turned to Colt and continued, "This time around, we'll need you to disable the electricity. You're on lookout duty as well."

Colt's fingers poked at the bandage on his shoulder with annoyance. Cain knew the big man was disappointed to be sidelined for the op, but he also knew he was a good Marine and would follow his orders to the end. Colt nodded his acceptance.

Cain shifted his attention to the rest of the team. "This operation requires every available hand. The entry team will consist of Swift, Woody, Flask and me. In light of recent events, everyone needs to be at their absolute best. We can't afford any screwups."

The three men nodded their comprehension.

"Colt," Cain continued, "you'll be our extract. Once we've made entry, double time back to the van and be prepared to move when needed."

Colt gave a lazy salute with his good hand.

Cain normally would have fired off a comment about disrespect, but respect was something he didn't have much of for himself lately, and therefore, it seemed off to request it from others. "Once we're inside, we're going weapons hot. This is not a knock and talk. We're hitting these guys like we're over in the sandpit. Copy?"

A volley of "Copy thats" and "Hell yeahs" followed. Cain was pleased to see the prospect of battle still brought his Marines to attention.

Cain rose from his seat and disappeared into the back room, returning moments later with a box brimming with clothes. "We're going to imper-sonate the delivery crew. The dealers that Gypsy's intercepting are affiliated with the Russian mob. We'll only have a couple seconds before they make us. We hit the external security hard using muzzle suppressors. No guarantee we're not going to draw attention from the men inside. The hope is we don't."

"Speed, surprise and violence of action." Flask delivered the entry credo with a wink.

"Hit 'em and forget 'em," Woody chimed in.

"What're the opposition numbers we're looking at for this run?" Flask asked.

"According to Gypsy," Cain continued, "there are seven men in total. Two guards, covering the outside. Plus, five total inside. The dealer keeps some heavy hitters close by his side, so once we're in, know we've got a fight on our hands." Cain turned to Swift. "Why don't you give a quick rundown of the layout based on your recon."

Swift toggled the mouse and manipulated the still shots of the target location. "The place is a two-story house. We've marked the garage as the primary entry point. Once inside, there's a short hall that connects to a kitchen. I was able to get these shots here through the side window. Looks like the stairwell is centered to the front door, splitting the first floor into two small rooms."

"Based on the intel provided by Gypsy, the second floor is where they keep the cash." Cain interrupted. "We're going in fingers crossed that they've already got the cash on the table in preparation for the deal. If not, Flask will have the det cord, and we'll breach the safe."

"I'll leave the video surveillance up so each of you can run through it a few times, so we all have a clear picture of the objective," Swift added.

"One last thing," Cain began, his tone more somber. "We've got some issues developing in regard to the fallout from our last op. Hatch is kicking the hornet's nest. She's become a real problem."

Silence hung in the air. Nobody spoke, but Cain could see the concern in each man's face. Behind the mask of bravado, they'd served in some of the harshest conditions, with death hiding around every corner. When Gypsy had come to him with the plan of taking some of the scourge of drugs off the street while lining their pockets, it had seemed like a no-brainer. In light of recent circumstances, it proved to be anything but. His men were hanging by a thread. One pull, and everything could come undone. It was his job to hold the line.

Cain looked at his rag-tag crew, hoping this mission would be their last. And after they'd cleared their trail, they could walk away. Some part of him doubted that, no matter how far he walked, the guilt he carried would ever leave him.

# THIRTY

EARLY THE NEXT MORNING, HATCH COMPLETED HER MORNING RITUAL OF running the streets around her motel in a three-mile loop. The sun had just begun to rise, but her clothes were soaked through as if she'd walked under a waterfall. Cooling off was an impossible task. Standing under the cold water of the shower had little effect. The minute she stepped out to towel off, her pores reopened the floodgates of perspiration.

Hatch embraced the suck factor and once again subjected herself to the brutal heat, deciding to make the walk, rather than drive, to Jimmy's Diner for her morning refueling. She wasn't sure where the day would take her, but preparation was ninety percent of the battle. The other percentage was focused determination, something Hatch had in ample supply.

Sophia's niece was excited to see her. She saw the hopeful look in her eyes as she strode past several waiting customers to greet Hatch. "Any news?"

Hatch controlled her response, reducing her cues of deception to a zero point. "Not yet." Hatch saw the impact her lie had, but she had a good reason to tell it. Exposing the fact that she'd located Sophia last night would potentially create an opening for anyone watching Sophia's friends and family. Louise would be an x-factor until Hatch resolved the situation.

Seeing the sadness in the young waitress's eyes, Hatch offered an emotional life preserver, "But I'm close. I can feel it. Just need a little more time."

"Thank you." Louise's dark cloud lifted, and the smile returned to her face. "Would you like the same as yesterday?"

"Sounds great." Hatch took a seat in a corner booth away from the other customers, keeping her back to the wall and facing out toward the door. With the information she'd gathered last night, her threat level had increased. "I heard you've got the best turtle pie around. That true?"

Louise's smile grew. "My dad's secret recipe."

"Your dad's Jimmy?"

She had a look of nostalgia with an edge of sadness. "He's gone now."

"Sorry to hear." Hatch offered a compassionate nod. "I'm sure he'd be proud you're still carrying the torch."

"My mom's been holding down the fort since his passing. My uncle was a big part of this place, but he's out of the picture now too."

"Is that your Aunt Sophia's husband?"

"Yup. He's supposed to get out of prison in the next day or so. Hopefully, he'll be in a better place, and we can get this diner runnin' like it used to. We'll see, I guess." She shrugged. "Hey, did you want a slice of the pie with your breakfast?"

"How 'bout I hold off. I'll treat myself when I get your aunt back safe and sound."

"You get my aunt back, and the pie's on the house." Louise spun and scurried back to the kitchen, fielding orders and coffee refill requests on the fly.

Hatch spent the remaining half hour consuming the ample breakfast and washing it down with copious amounts of coffee before setting off for her next objective. She read the time on her watch. Just past 8:30AM, midafternoon by military standards. Hatch hopped into her rental car and drove toward Naval Air Station Panama City.

A Marine Military Policeman stood guard at the gated entrance. As Hatch pulled to a stop, he greeted her with the professionalism she'd come to expect. He asked for her identification. Hatch presented him with her military ID. He inspected it carefully, his body a rigid statue impervious to the beating sun.

"Army?"

Hatch gave a nod.

"MOS?"

The military occupation specialty is a common question among servicemembers. It's a way of gauging another's experience. Hatch offered a half-smile. "Same as you. That's where I cut my teeth, anyway."

"Says here you're retired?" The Marine was still holding onto her ID card.

"Medical."

He looked at her, weighing the information and then noticing the scar. He handed the card back. "Thank you for your service. Mind if I ask your business on base today?"

"I'm heading to speak with NCIS Agent Granger."

"He expecting you?"

"I don't think so. I'm following up on Gunnery Sergeant Ryker's death."

The Marine MP gave a solemn nod. "Damn shame, that was."

"No doubt about that." Hatch thought of all the other shame that was soon to be exposed. It sickened her.

"Need me to call ahead for you?"

"Not necessary."

The MP rattled off directions to the NCIS office. He then struck a salute before waving her through.

She parked in front. Only one other car was parked out front, a beat-up Volkswagen Beetle. Hatched stepped inside the small office. The air conditioning was on full blast, shocking her system. A woman sat behind the desk to the side of the small waiting room. She wore a light sweater for reasons obvious to Hatch. The setup, although smaller than the Hawk's Landing Sheriff's Office, was similar in design with the reception area cordoned off from the office area.

"May I help you, Miss?"

"I'm here to see Agent Granger."

"Not in yet." There was an edge to her voice.

Hatch looked at the clock on the wall. It read 9:15. Late by the standards engrained into her for the last fifteen-plus years. "Is he planning on coming in?"

"I assume so. Probably running late." She gave a shrug. "It happens sometimes."

Hatch nodded. She looked out toward the lot. Seeing no sign of any approaching vehicle, she considered leaving with the intent of trying again later. Problem was, Granger could possibly be in the best position to assist in developing a case against Hurley and his men.

"Feel free to wait. Coffee's not too bad, if you're in the mood."

"I never turn down a cup." Hatch moved over to the small table where the pot's escaping vapors added its aroma to the surroundings. She was pouring herself a cup when the front door opened. A tall, thin man with unkempt salt-and-pepper hair stepped inside, trailed by a Jetstream of hot air.

"Beau, got yourself a visitor this morning." The receptionist motioned to Hatch. "I forgot to get your name."

"Rachel Hatch."

Granger eyed her and offered a reserved smile. "What can I do you for?"

"I'm an old friend of Gunnery Sergeant Jeff Ryker."

His eyes darkened. "Terrible tragedy."

"That's what I wanted to speak with you about."

"Not much I can discuss. Security protocols, you know."

"Guess I'll be the one doing the talking then."

"Not sure I catch your drift." Granger pushed back his hair from his forehead.

"I've got some information you might deem relevant to your investigation." Hatch looked around the small lobby. "Mind if we speak privately?"

Granger let out a deep sigh before gesturing toward the door. "Follow me to my office."

Hatch walked with Granger, taking up stride a half step behind the lanky investigator. In his wake, she thought she caught the faint odor of stale liquor. They came to a closed door on the left. The placard identified it as his office.

The interior was sparse, containing a desk, a few chairs, and a bookcase filled with an equal number of books and military memorabilia. Hatch caught sight of a picture. In it a younger, sharper-looking version of Granger stood outside a helicopter.

"You were a pilot?"

"Long time ago. Don't look the part of a Marine these days." He chuckled softly to himself and mussed his hair. "Civilian life, I guess. NCIS may fall under the Department of the Navy, but the agents aren't military. I've reverted to the pre-service hippie look of my youth. Though the hair's got a lot grayer since then."

"It's been an adjustment for me as well." Hatch offered an obligatory smile.

"I'm guessing you didn't come to discuss my life story or my hair. What is it that you wanted to share with me?"

"I received a call from Ryker before he died. He was distraught. Next day, I get here to find he's dead."

"And you think the two are related?"

"I've got reason to suspect there's plenty of things in play here. None of which are good."

Granger took out a pad and pen. "Why don't you give me everything and let me sort through it?"

Hatch spent the next twenty minutes explaining the facts she'd uncovered since first arriving at Panama City. She connected the dots between Santiago's investigation and the link she'd made to First Sergeant Hurley and his men.

After concluding, Granger let out an exhausted groan. "You've given me a hell of a lot to process. I'm gonna need some time to corroborate the information. What you're suggesting carries a lot of implications for some very decorated Marines."

"Is that going to be a problem for you?"

Granger leveled a no-nonsense glare at Hatch. "Once a Marine, always a Marine. That said, I'm an investigator through and through. And I see my cases to the end, regardless of where they take me."

"Fair enough." Hatch stood and shook Granger's hand. "Thank you for your time. I can see myself out."

"Hatch, let me do my job." He cocked his head to the side, looking up from his desk at her under his bushy eyebrows. "I'll see it through."

"Glad to hear it. Do that, and you probably won't be seeing me again."

Hatch exited the office, closing the door behind her. She said goodbye to the receptionist, escaping the air-conditioned tundra for the thick mugginess awaiting her in the parking lot.

As she headed off of the base, Hatch caught sight of a group of Marines training on the tarmac. She recognized one who stood out from the rest. A large Marine with his arm in a sling was barking orders at a group of trainees.

Seeing one of Hurley's men gave her an idea. She'd been advised by Granger to let it rest while he worked the case. But Hatch was never good about idle hands. She prepared to put them to use in the interim. She pulled off to the side, using a building for cover as she waited and watched.

She rolled down the window. A warm breeze entered, carrying a hint of rain. The clouds in the distance darkened. A storm approached. Hatch hoped it wasn't the one Tracy had predicted.

# THIRTY-ONE

HATCH WAITED IN THE SWELTER OF THE MIDDAY SUN. SHE CONTINUED TO watch Staff Sergeant Brunson, his right arm cradled in a sling, lead the young Marines before him with an unwavering intensity. Around him, the trainees followed his every command, the training exercises testing not only their physical prowess but also their mental resolve.

The distant thump of helicopter blades cut through the air, a rhythmic beat that pulsed through Hatch, calling forth the memory of Ryker and his tragic death. As the helicopter drew closer, Brunson barked orders to the anxious Marines.

The helicopter roared into position, hovering just above the ground. Staff Sergeant Brunson signaled for the trainees to enter. One by one, they sprinted to the aircraft. Others maintained ground security. Hand and arm signals dictated the movements. Within less than a minute, ten Marines had entered the helicopter before it lifted off once more. The drill repeated until each group had completed several rotations.

When a Marine trainee made a mistake, Brunson was quick to dish out a punishment that was equal parts inventive and grueling. Hatch understood that pain was a powerful teacher, and that the ache in their muscles would serve as the penalty of failure.

Hatch's mind drifted back to her own arduous journey, and the relentless gauntlet she had run to become the first female to complete the Army's elite Special Forces Q-Course. Beyond that, she'd been hand-picked as a member of the secret unit, Task Force Banshee, which eventually brought about tragedy, propelling her in a new direction, one that put her on the path she was on now. Its end remained unknown. All of it had molded her into the hardened, unyielding warrior she was today.

As Hatch waited for Brunson to wrap up the recruit training, she placed a call to Jordan Tracy. She kept her gaze fixed on the training grounds where the Marine Staff Sergeant continued his unrelenting command of the exhausted recruits, pushing them to their limits.

While she waited, Hatch placed a quick call to Renee. She asked for the names and ranks of the men her husband had served with in the training unit. She jotted them down and did her best to assure Renee it was nothing to worry about before ending the call. Hatch wasn't sure the Marine widow believed her.

With the list in hand, Hatch dialed another number, one that she had come to rely on more than she'd ever intended during the past couple of days.

"Tracy," he answered.

Hatch heard the unspoken 'what now?' tone of his voice. "Hate asking. But I need your help again."

"What's going on? This is becoming more concerning with each call."

"I know. The more I dig, the deeper things get."

"Par for the course with you." Tracy let out a frustrated exhale. "What's up?"

"I've got some names," Hatch replied, her gaze lingering on Staff Sergeant Brunson. "I need you to run a check on these men. Anything pertinent, I'm going to need ASAP."

"What would you deem pertinent?"

"Maybe a ding or two in their service record. Something that might shed light on why they got caught up in this. I'm just trying to wrap my head around all of this and make sense of it."

"Is this related to the woman you asked me to find earlier?"

"Yes. She was a witness to the double homicide. The information she provided me confirms it was Hurley and his men. Proving it beyond her statement is what I'm working on."

"All right. I've come to trust your judgment. As much as I don't like digging up dirt on our military brethren, sounds like this is one of those that absolutely warrants it."

"These men—they served with Ryker. They were there when he died."

"You're saying his death was no accident?"

"Looks that way."

"Give me the names you want me to run. I'll see what I can do."

Hatch listed the names. Marine First Sergeant Hurley, Staff Sergeant Greg Brunson, Staff Sergeant James Woodrow, Sergeant Roger Kastner, and Sergeant Mark Li—these were the men who held the key to the truth she so desperately sought.

"I know what I'm asking you is a lot. But these men are no longer Marines. They're a ruthless gang capable of running military-style hits on local drug dealers and robbing them of their cash."

"Give me a few hours. I'll see what I can dig up." Tracy paused for a moment. When he continued again, his voice crackled with concern. "I'm worried this might be too much for you to handle alone. After your last request, I made the executive decision to have backup on standby. And now, after hearing what you're in the middle of, I'm sending Banyan your way."

"But—"

"No choice in the matter," Tracy said, cutting her off. "You're a Talon asset now. And we protect our assets."

Hatch clenched her jaw, her pride flaring, but she knew better than to continue her challenge. She'd pushed too far, and Tracy's rationale was based on reasoning she couldn't argue with.

"Fine," she relented. "Send him."

Tracy's voice softened. "He'll be there in a couple of hours. Lay low until he arrives. Let local law enforcement work the problem."

"Seems to be a bit of a snag on their end. The detective I've made contact with hasn't been answering my calls. Not sure why, but the dead air is disconcerting." She paused. "But there's someone else. NCIS Agent Beau

Granger. He's the investigator responsible for the initial review of Ryker's death. I filled him in on Hurley and his men. Let him know about the possible implication that Ryker's death was no accident. He's looking into it."

"Well, I've got my marching orders. So do you," Tracy said, "Let's do our parts and hopefully this thing will come to a satisfactory resolution soon. One that doesn't require any more bloodshed."

"I'd like nothing more. But if the past dictates the future, I'm not making any promises."

"That may be true." Tracy accompanied his words with a soft chuckle. "At least your percentage of seeing through whatever comes of it are, to put mildly, off the charts."

"Let's hope I can keep it that way."

Hatch pressed her thumb down on the glowing red button on her phone, severing her connection to Jordan Tracy. The sense of urgency grew as she watched Marine Staff Sergeant Brunson wrap up the day's training session.

The sun dipped low in the sky, casting long shadows across the base. The air had taken on a cooler edge, but Hatch could still feel the heat radiating. She maintained her position, watching Brunson walk with a sense of purpose toward his Jeep. The fading light caught on his close-cropped hair, the sweat on his brow a testament to the hard hours of training.

As Brunson got into his Jeep, Hatch slipped her rental car from behind the cover where she'd sat most of the day. She fought to keep her eyes on his vehicle while maintaining a safe distance, determined not to be noticed. The engine hummed beneath her, a steady rhythm in the tense silence.

She trailed him as he exited the base, careful to remain far enough back that he wouldn't suspect he was being followed. The Jeep's taillights glowed like a beacon in the growing darkness, guiding her through the winding roads that led them away from the military facility. They were headed toward the outskirts of Panama City, the urban sprawl giving way to a more rural landscape.

Nestled at the edge of the city limits, the property appeared unassuming at first glance. A small, one-story structure with a modest yard blended seamlessly with the surrounding homes. But Hatch knew better than to be deceived by its innocuous appearance. She parked her car a safe distance away, her gaze locked on the Jeep as it pulled into the driveway.

Brunson stepped out of his vehicle, glancing around the quiet neighborhood before disappearing into the house. Hatch's pulse quickened as she considered her next move. She knew she had to be cautious, yet swift. She knew the clock was ticking and time was not on her side.

With a deep, steadying breath, Hatch slipped out of her car and into the fading light. She moved with the precision of a predator, finding a spot beside a shed, covered by a thick nest of trees. The evening breeze rustled the leaves overhead, providing her with the perfect cover to watch the house, as she stood invisible in the shadows.

# THIRTY-TWO

THE SUN DIPPED TOWARD THE HORIZON, BUT THE THICK, HUMID AIR CLUNG to Santiago as she struggled with her mother's ancient window air conditioning unit. Her shirt clung to her back, slick with sweat. This was the kind of heat she had grown accustomed to, but it had been a long time since she'd felt so trapped by it.

"Damn thing," she muttered under her breath, setting the screwdriver aside in frustration. She knew her annoyance wasn't directed at the stubborn appliance, but at the circumstances that had led her here. The suspension, the argument with Captain Parnell, and the knowledge that she'd crossed the line with Malcolm's case. It ate at her, like the oppressive heat bearing down on her now.

Her mother appeared in the doorway with a glass of water and a beer. Santiago took the water, downing it in one long gulp, before reaching for the beer. She tried to read her mother's face, but the expression was carefully neutral. She knew her mother was secretly glad she'd been suspended, hoping that this would be the end of her dangerous career.

Their relationship had been strained over the years, with Santiago interpreting her mother's worry as nagging. But now, as they stood together in the small house, the normal bickering seemed to have been put on hold. Santiago could see the concern in her mother's eyes, but she also saw something else. Hope.

The quiet moment stretched between them, and Santiago found herself feeling vulnerable. She took a deep breath, her hand gripping the beer a little too tightly.

"Mom," she began. "I know you think I'm better off not being a cop, but it's who I am."

"I know, mija, but I can't help but worry. I just want you to be safe."

"I always do my best."

"You just remind me so much of your father." Her mother's voice broke as she choked back tears.

"Stubbornness runs in the genes." Santiago smiled, and for a moment, the tension between them eased.

"Let's hope it doesn't carry to Isabella."

As the sun set and the heat began to dissipate, they stood together, the broken air conditioner momentarily forgotten. In this fragile peace, Santiago felt the weight of her past decisions and the uncertainty of her future, but she also felt the love and support of her mom. And maybe, that would be enough to carry her through.

Santiago leaned back in the worn armchair in her mother's living room, her eyes tracing the familiar pattern of the wallpaper, a soothing mixture of warm browns and oranges. Santiago's cell phone vibrated, startling her. The screen displayed an unexpected name: Orson, the forensic tech from Bay County Lab. She caught a look from her mother, causing Santiago to hesitate a fraction of a second before answering.

"Hey, Orson. What's up?" Santiago tried to sound casual, as if she hadn't just been suspended.

"I called the station, but I couldn't reach you at your desk. Sorry for calling your cell after hours," Orson stammered, his voice soft and apologetic.

"No problem," Santiago replied. "Did you find anything?"

Santiago saw her mother's ears perk up as she tried to eavesdrop on the conversation. Noticing her mother's interest, Santiago rose from the chair and retreated to the kitchen, seeking some semblance of privacy.

"Yeah, I did," Orson said, excitement creeping into his voice. "Belongs to a Greg Brunson. He was arrested for assault a few years back. I did some digging, and it turns out he's a Marine stationed at the base in Panama City."

Santiago's heart raced, her thoughts swirling like a storm. Being suspended, she would have had difficulty pulling this information herself.

"Thank you, Orson. I appreciate your help," Santiago said. "I owe you one."

"No problem," Orson replied. "I'll see if I can take you up on owing me sometime."

The call ended, and Santiago stared at the phone for a moment, her pulse still racing. She should report the information to her superiors, but she couldn't just waltz back into the precinct. As Santiago walked back into the living room, her mother's eyes met hers.

"What's going on, mija?" Rosa asked, her voice a mixture of concern and curiosity, the lines of worry and concern carving her face like an artist's chisel.

"Just some work stuff," she said, attempting to sound nonchalant. "Nothing to worry about."

Rosa's eyebrows shot up, disbelief laced with a hint of anger. "Work? You were suspended from the force earlier today. What could they possibly want from you?"

Santiago swallowed hard, searching for a plausible explanation. "It's related to an old case, Mamá. They needed my input. That's all."

Rosa held her daughter's gaze, her eyes searching for the truth. But after a moment, she sighed and relented. "Very well." Her voice softened as she gestured toward the kitchen. "Come help me with dinner. It's been far too long since we've cooked together."

Santiago acquiesced, her heart heavy with guilt. She could not remember the last time she had shared this simple pleasure with her mother. As she began to reach for a knife, Rosa turned and called out, "Isabella! Ven aquí, mi amor! Join us in the kitchen!"

The sound of the young girl's laughter floated into the room as Santiago's heart clenched, torn between duty and family. "Mamá, I need to make a quick call."

Rosa's face tightened, annoyance settling like a storm cloud over her features. "Don't be too long."

Isabella's bright eyes sparkled as she entered the room, her youth and innocence a stark contrast to the shadows clinging to Santiago's soul. As she watched her daughter join Rosa at the counter, Santiago slipped from the room.

Santiago's thumb hovered over the screen, ready to dial Rachel Hatch's number, when her phone buzzed with an incoming call. The number was blocked. She hesitated, contemplating letting it go to voicemail, but something compelled her to answer.

"Yeah?" she said, her voice a guarded mix of curiosity and irritation.

A raspy, gruff voice spoke from the other end. "I'm looking for Detective Santiago."

She hesitated for a moment, then replied, "You found her."

"This is NCIS Agent Beau Granger," he said. "I hear you're working the double homicide."

Santiago didn't bother correcting him. Malcolm was technically in charge, but that didn't matter now. She'd just gotten information linking the murders to a Marine. "That's right," she said, playing along.

There was a pause on the other end. "That's why I'm calling. I think there's more to this story. But I don't want to talk over the phone. Can we meet?"

Santiago glanced over at her mother and daughter, busy prepping the kitchen for dinner. "When?"

"Now," Granger said.

She hesitated, then agreed. He gave her an address and hung up.

Santiago returned to the kitchen. Her mother gave her a questioning look, which turned to disappointment when she said, "I've got to step out for a minute."

"Is this about your job?" her mother asked.

Santiago didn't answer. Instead, she leaned down and kissed her daughter on the head. "I'll be right back," she promised.

Her mother sighed. "You always say that, but you never keep your promises."

The words stung, but Santiago brushed them off. This case had consumed her for the better part of a year, causing both professional and personal turmoil. She couldn't let it go now, not when she was so close to solving it.

As she left the house, the last rays of the sun dipped below the horizon. She climbed into her car and headed toward the meeting spot, her heart racing with anticipation and anxiety. Whatever Agent Granger had to say, it was bound to change everything.

# THIRTY-THREE

HATCH SHIFTED HER WEIGHT, HER MUSCLES TENSE AND READY FOR ACTION AS she kept her eyes fixed on the unremarkable house on the outskirts of Panama City. She could feel the oppressive humidity sticking to her skin, but she barely noticed it.

The sun had long since dipped below the horizon, casting a dark veil over the landscape. Shadows deepened, and the scent of damp earth mingled with the salt of the nearby gulf. She'd spent the day tracking Brunson. She'd hoped for a break in the case, but so far, her efforts had yielded nothing.

As she stood in her hiding spot behind a shed, shrouded by the protective embrace of the trees, Hatch contemplated her next move. With the night settling in, she considered retreating to the safety of her motel room to rest and regroup, ready to resume her vigil the next day.

Hatch gave herself a few more minutes, her fingers drumming a silent rhythm against the tree she was tucked behind. She was about to slip away when headlights sliced through the darkness, immediately followed by two others. They rolled to a stop in front of the house Brunson had entered.

She recognized the familiar faces of Sergeants Kastner, Li, and Woodrow as they stepped out. Her pulse quickened, her instincts screaming that something was unfolding before her eyes. The pieces were coming together, the puzzle forming a picture that was both so close yet still out of reach.

She held her breath and watched, her senses sharpened by the adrenaline coursing through her veins. She knew she couldn't leave now, not when the stakes were this high. She was on the verge of discovering the truth, of unearthing the secrets that had claimed the lives of innocent people and had shattered those impacted in the wake of tragedy, people like Renee and her daughter, and Sophia and her children.

As the men trickled into the house, Hatch made a decision. She would stay, watch, and wait. Observe and report was her current mission. She intended on keeping it that way. The past dictated some things were out of her control. Hatch hoped this wasn't one of them.

Hatch pulled out her phone, scrolling through her contacts until she found the number for Detective Santiago. She hesitated for a moment before hitting the call button. The line rang. She'd already left Santiago a voicemail earlier, but felt compelled to try to reach her again, to update her on the evolving situation.

After the third ring went unanswered, Hatch slid her thumb to end the call when she heard Santiago's voice. "Santiago."

"It's Hatch. I've been running down some leads."

"I'm listening."

"I think I've got a lock on who's been doing those robberies. The same men responsible for the double homicide." Hatch paused. Even though everything in her gut pointed in this direction, saying it out loud stung. It was a betrayal of the honor she'd always held for those who served. In light of recent events, the blind adoration was now tempered with the harsh reality that people were people, regardless of position. "It's about First Sergeant Hurley and the members of his training unit. I think they're the ones responsible."

"I know." Santiago breathed heavily into the other end.

"You knew this?" Hatch asked.

"I didn't. Not until a few minutes ago."

"Problem on my end is that Sophia's eyewitness testimony isn't likely to be enough to put these guys away. It's circumstantial at best."

"Not anymore. I pulled a blood sample from the stairwell. Lab results just came back to a Greg Brunson, a Marine on base here."

"He's one of Hurley's crew." Hatch watched the house. The silhouette of one of the men was illuminated by the light from within. "You might want to join me."

"Why's that?"

"I'm outside of a house I saw him enter not too long ago."

"You're tailing these guys?"

"I told you. I don't stop until I'm satisfied."

"Sounds like you and I aren't so different."

"Not a bad thing. But I'm a bit biased."

"I won't be able to make it right now. I'm on my way to meet with an NCIS agent by the name of Granger."

"I spoke with him earlier. He's aware of what's going on. I guess he must've found a connection."

"You held up your end by keeping me in the loop. I'll do the same once I find out what Granger's got."

"Well, whatever you two talk about, you might want to make it quick. Because three others just arrived. Waiting on Hurley to show."

"If something breaks bad, call the department. Ask to speak with Captain Parnell. If he's not in, they can connect you to his cell." Santiago's voice lowered. "He's the only one I trust right now."

"Are you saying what I think you're saying?" Hatch asked.

"It's been a theory I've had for a while. This crew has managed to dodge me at every pass for the past year. I'm not perfect, but my record speaks for itself. My case closure rate is second to none at my PD. Yet, other than the last six months, I haven't been able to get close enough for even a sniff at who might be behind it."

"If what you're alluding to is correct, there's a big problem."

"It's got to be a cop. No other way I can see it. Someone's able to manipulate cases. Hell, he's probably the one picking the targets, too."

"Any ideas on who it might be?"

"Nothing solid. But if you put a gun to my head, I'd put my money on Detective Malcolm. He's running the double murder. Might be why I've hit so many roadblocks." Santiago grunted. "He's damn sure responsible for my suspension."

"Suspension?"

"Earlier today. They put me out."

"For what?" Hatch was perplexed. Everything she'd gleaned from her limited exposure to Santiago told her that she was a stalwart and tenacious investigator.

"What they called interfering, I call it police work. Guess they didn't see it that way."

"Doesn't seem like their suspension stopped you."

"When met with an impasse, I believe in finding a way around."

"Sounds like I can assist in that regard," Hatch said. "I'll be your eyes. I can relay pertinent information to your captain."

"I appreciate it."

"Don't thank me yet." Hatch eyed the house. "We've still got to bring them down. And from where I stand, these guys seem to be building to something. Maybe working on their next score."

"I'm almost to the location Granger gave me. I'll touch base after." Santiago remained on the line a moment longer. "Stay put. Don't go trying to stop these guys yourself."

"People keep telling me that." Hatch thought of Tracy and the similar warning he'd given her. "But I'm not so good at letting things go."

"You and I both. Let's just hope it doesn't send us to an early grave." Santiago ended the call.

Hatch stood in the fading light, the weight of the revelation settling on her shoulders. She knew there would be no turning back now. Night descended upon Panama City, but Hatch was just getting started.

# THIRTY-FOUR

HURLEY SAT IN HIS TRUCK, DESPERATELY WISHING HE'D REFILLED HIS FLASK, still resting on the floorboard where he'd thrown it in frustration the other day. His mounting tension had only grown over the last twenty-four hours. Sweat beaded on his brow, a mixture of anxiety and the oppressive heat that hung in the stagnant air.

Long shadows seemed to claw at Hurley's conscience. He wished for the comfort of the amber liquid that had once filled his flask, its metallic surface reflecting the anger that had coursed through him when he'd tossed it to the floorboard. He wanted to dull the edges of his nerves, but none of it would change the gravity of the situation.

Gypsy's voice echoed in his mind, the words a haunting melody: a remedy, a solution to their impending doom. Hurley knew there would be no turning back. He was now a crucial element in a desperate gambit, one that would either save them all or send them spiraling into the abyss. The outcome rested on his shoulders, and he would carry it into the darkness awaiting them.

The disappointment of the news regarding their upcoming op was outweighed by the need for personal preservation. No amount of money would matter if they spent the rest of their lives in prison, something that would surely be the case if they were caught. Gypsy had come up with a remedy to that problem. Hurley was an integral part of the solution.

Hurley thought of his men at the safehouse. They were a well-oiled machine, methodically preparing for the next job – checking their gear, running the final surveillance, and gearing up for the hit that would change their lives. They were counting on him, and would begin to worry about his tardiness, so he picked up the phone and dialed Brunson's number.

"Cain, we've been waiting on your word. Any problems on your end?"

"We can drop the call signs now." Hurley hesitated for a moment before saying, "It's time to go underground."

"We've put too much into this, Hurley. This is the one that could set us up for life, the one that could let us walk away from all this." Brunson didn't bother hiding his disappointment.

Under normal circumstances, had any Marine spoken to him with such an attitude in their tone, he would've made them regret the day they were born. This was no longer the case. The undeniable respect afforded during his career didn't transfer to whatever it was he'd become. And over the past few days, it had hit an all-time low.

"Doesn't matter. Gypsy called the op. It's done. Nothing we can do about it." Hurley knew the stakes, but he also knew the risks. "All that money won't matter if we're locked away and can't spend it, Brunson."

Silence hung in the air for a moment, and then Brunson asked, "So, what's the plan?"

"I've got a move in play to take care of the threats against us," Hurley replied, the certainty in his voice masking the unease in his gut. "I've put you and the rest of the crew on leave. After tonight, we all need to disappear for a few weeks, lay low until things cool down."

"When do we need to get out of here?"

"Now," Hurley said, his voice carrying the urgency of their situation.

With that, he ended the call, leaving Brunson and his men to follow his order while Hurley prepared for the next step in clearing any trace.

One of their problems was already locked in the trunk, the cacophony of muffled protests and desperate gasps having finally given way to quiet. The next was still out there, and Hurley knew this was just the beginning of a long and brutal night. Hurley looked toward the darkness in front of him. The orange tip flared with each drag from Gypsy's cigarette.

The first half of their problems lay silenced in the trunk of the car. The second half, however, still needed to be dealt with.

The silence was broken by the hum of a vehicle approaching. The moment they had been waiting for had arrived, and there was no turning back.

Gypsy crushed the cigarette under his boot, the orange glow winking out as the darkness reclaimed its territory.

As he waited for the target to come into view, Hurley knew there was no room for hesitation. This would be the most difficult part. And he wasn't about to let his guard down. The hardened Marine prepared for the most important battle of his life.

# THIRTY-FIVE

HATCH FOLLOWED THE INSTRUCTIONS GRANGER HAD GIVEN HER. THE DRIVE took a little over the twenty minutes he'd estimated. As she reached the abandoned warehouse, her headlights danced across the graffiti-covered walls. Most of the windows were broken. The fencing around the lot was rusted, part of which was flattened under the weight of a collapsed tree.

She didn't see any sign of Granger or Santiago and began to question whether she'd gotten the information wrong. Hatch was about to place a call to Granger when she caught sight of a white four-door sedan parked at the back end of the building.

Hatch pulled into the parking lot. The gravel-covered dirt crackled and popped as she moved forward. As she passed the dark opening of what was at one point the front door to the business, an orange glow, like that of a firefly, caught her eye. The embers of the cigarette revealed the gaunt features of Agent Granger.

He flicked the butt and stepped from the shadows. Granger flashed a wave.

Hatch brought the rental to a stop. Granger ambled toward her and was already in the process of digging another cigarette from his pack when Hatch rolled the window down. "Didn't see you there."

"That's why I like this place."

"I thought you said Santiago was here." Hatch scanned her surroundings, seeing no sign of the detective.

"She is. Over there." Ganger pointed toward the white car with the end of his unlit cigarette. "Figured I'd flag you down. Guide you to the spot."

"Okay." Hatch put the car in park.

"Why don't you pull it around back where she's parked?" Granger looked around, surveying the area around the lot. He leaned in toward the Cruiser's open window. "I know. You probably think all this cloak and dagger's a bit overkill. Been doin' this awhile. Old habits die hardest."

"Trust me, I get it." Hatch did as he requested. She drove slowly. No need to kick up dust for the man ambling behind. The orange firefly lagged in the rearview mirror.

Hatch rounded the corner. She pulled around the white Ford Taurus parked along the corner. A few spaces down was a light green Chevrolet Caprice with government tags, identifying the vehicle as Granger's. She split the difference, pulling between them.

As she exited the vehicle, Hatch saw no sign of Santiago. Granger walked into view. "Where's Santiago?"

"She mentioned having to use the bathroom. Must've slipped off to find some privacy." He shrugged and offered a smile. "When nature calls, it's best to answer."

"Guess so." Hatch felt the quietness of their surroundings. Granger picked a good spot as far as privacy went.

"Why don't we compare notes while we're waiting on the detective to return?"

"Sure thing. Why don't you tell me where you're at, and I'll see if I can shed some light."

"I did some digging into what you said earlier." He scratched the stubble on his chin and then pushed back a greasy wisp of hair that had fallen across his face. "The timelines of the robberies appear to be synchronized with the dates Ryker's wife gave you. Problem is, that's not going to hold in court. It's conjecture. Easy to interpret as coincidence."

"That's why I gave it to you. Grab a search warrant and pull the phone records for Hurley and his men. Communications could add weight.

Might even get cell tower data to put them on location at the date and time of the robberies."

Granger gave a slow nod. His fingers played with an unlit cigarette, rolling it between his index and middle finger. "Might work. That is, if they're dumb enough to use their personal cells for something like this. But I think you would agree, these men aren't your average criminals. They have worked in some of the most hostile environments in the world."

"You make a fair point." Hatch scanned the surrounding darkness, looking for the detective. "Santiago had some leads. Blood evidence. That'll hold weight in court."

Granger's eyes squinted. "She did mention it. Seemed to have some potential."

"Have some potential? That blood puts Brunson on scene at the time of the double murder." Hatch cocked an eyebrow. "That's not potential. That's a prosecutor's dream come true."

"Not from where I stand." Granger stopped fidgeting with the cigarette. Instead of lighting it, he tucked it behind his ear. "Not sure if Santiago mentioned to you, but she was suspended earlier today."

Hatch nodded, understanding where the agent was headed and feeling the wind sucked from her sails. "She told me."

"Did she tell you that she collected the evidence on her own? That she wasn't assigned to the case, and that she was actually restricted from any involvement in the investigation?"

"The way she tells it, the detective assigned to the case isn't pulling his weight." Hatch opted not to mention Santiago's suspicions about her coworker's actions being deliberate. She could see Granger wasn't pleased with Santiago's methods and didn't want to build a case against her. "He missed an opportunity to process a critical piece of evidence."

"Do you think a jury will see it that way?"

"They will when the DNA matches Staff Sergeant Brunson's."

"My guess is that evidence will never see the light of day. Any defense attorney worth a damn would bury it deep during a suppression hearing. The method of evidence collection is just as important as the evidence collected."

"I'm not sure you're right."

"Not sure?" Granger shook his head. "This isn't a game. This case will have ripple effects that go far beyond the victims. This gets out, the entire Marine Corps goes on trial. You do understand that, right?"

"I do." Hatch leaned against the driver's door of her rental car. "I also understand that there are bad people in honorable jobs. The actions of the few do not reflect that of the many."

"Maybe. Maybe not. The point is, for this case to withstand that level of scrutiny, it's got to be airtight."

"Then what is it you're looking for?"

"The witness." Granger folded his arms across his chest. "Santiago said you've spoken to her."

Hatch felt uneasy. She'd made a promise to Sophia, one that carried over to her two young boys. But she also knew the power of her testimony, something Hatch hoped wouldn't be needed. After listening to Granger, she was hard pressed to see another alternative to gaining traction with this case. Sophia's sworn statement would open the door for the other evidence. It would tighten the case and improve the chances of an effective prosecution of Hurley and his men.

"So, did you or did you not speak with her?"

"I did."

"Yet, when we spoke today, you made no mention of it." Granger's voice was edgier now.

"I made her a promise." Hatch pushed off the car, her body rigid. "And that's something I don't take lightly."

"Are you willing to let your promise jeopardize our chance of bringing these guys to justice?"

Hatch met the agent's gaze. "Tell me what you need."

"I need to speak with her."

"I'll see what I can do."

"I don't think you get it." Granger kicked the gravel at his feet. "You're not in any capacity to make this case. You've got zero jurisdiction. You're an outsider looking in."

"Sophia is afraid. With good reason. I don't think she's going to agree to speak about this to you or anyone else."

"It's worth a shot. If she's able to put what she saw into writing, I just might be able to salvage this cluster. To do that, I'm going to need to know where she's at." Granger slipped the cigarette from behind his ear and stuck it in his mouth. "Gonna help me with that?"

Hatch let out a slow exhale. She gave Granger the motel's address, where Sophia and her children were staying. She asked to go with him to meet with her, hoping to mitigate any fallout from the promise she'd broken. She planned to lay out the importance of her eyewitness testimony to the raid and Ryker's contact with her afterward. Granger agreed.

She'd been so focused on the interaction with Granger, Hatch realized Santiago still hadn't returned. Her vision had adjusted to the darkness, but the improvement hadn't given her a visual of the detective anywhere in the proximity of where they stood.

"Thank you." Granger brought the lighter up to the end of his cigarette. His thumb sat poised on the striker.

"Just glad to help."

"You've been a bigger help than you'll ever know." He flicked the lighter, casting his face in the glow of the flame. He took a deep drag, blowing the smoke out of the side of his mouth, he said, "Now, I'm gonna need you to do one more thing."

Hatch heard the sound of footsteps on gravel. She turned, expecting to see Santiago returning. Instead, she was shocked to see First Sergeant Calvin Hurley materialize out of the darkness, even more so by the fact he was holding a Glock semi-automatic pistol pointed in her direction.

# THIRTY-SIX

THICK CLOUDS FORMED ABOVE. THE GRAY MASSES SPARKED WITH LIGHTNING, foretelling of the coming storm. The rain had yet to fall, but Hatch was already drenched in the sweat oozing from her pores.

She processed the situation unraveling before her. Hatch calculated her response. The weapon was centered on Hatch's torso. Hurley was only twelve feet away. If the gun had still been holstered, like Granger's was, she could have crossed the distance before it was drawn. Under the circumstances, the movement would likely result in certain death. Calculating odds in a millisecond was as important to survival as having the requisite skills needed for such an encounter.

She picked up Granger out of the corner of her eye. He was closer, and the weaker of the two, but it didn't change the fact that Hurley had his weapon trained on her. Running the numbers, Hatch came up on the losing end.

Hatch selected the best option when facing unbeatable odds. Stall. And hope that the window of time will provide the opportunity to improve them.

She raised her hands slowly, bringing them to shoulder height. Unlike when Santiago had confronted her outside of Sophia's apartment, Hurley had a murderous intent in his eyes, the sight of which was disconcerting for Hatch.

"So, what's the play, gentlemen?" Hatch asked, her voice steady, her mind sharp.

"You don't give up do you? Still looking for your angle of opportunity?" Granger asked.

"Always." Hatch's face curled into a snarl. "Give me the opportunity, and you're both dead before your bodies hit the ground."

"Told you she was the real deal." Hurley chuckled. "Don't let your guard down around this one for a second. Not like the cop."

Hatch's thoughts turned to Santiago. "Where is she?"

"Don't worry. You'll be with her soon," Granger said. After taking a long pull from the cigarette, he dropped it to the ground and crushed it into the gravel beneath his shoe. He exhaled, the smoke leaving his mouth as he continued speaking. "We didn't want it to come to this. But you really left no choice in the matter."

"I'm not sure how you plan to spin this, but there's no way adding more bodies to the count will benefit you."

"True. But Santiago's already assisted in that matter." Granger never took his eyes off Hatch. "She's convinced that Detective Malcolm was dirty. Or at least, she was convinced, until about a half hour ago. She even went so far as to make the accusation to her superior prior to her suspension. No, it's just a matter of connecting those dots."

"You're out of your mind," Hatch said, fighting to contain the rage filling her body. Unchecked, it could spill over to action. And anger never helped the odds.

"Maybe. I guess time will tell. Your time is nearing its end, but don't you worry, I'll be around to assist in making sure things line up with the investigation." Granger smiled. "You were pretty upset at the death of your friend. You pushed the investigation, even convinced Detective Santiago to follow you down the rabbit hole."

"Doesn't change the fact Brunson's blood's on the scene. You can't dodge that."

"Already have. Remember? We went through this. I just needed to secure the last piece capable of turning the tide."

"Sophia," Hatch muttered under her breath.

"That's right. With her out of the picture, everything else is a walk in the park. And I'd like to thank you for locating her." Granger looked at Hurley. "Brunson and the others should be on their way to take care of that little bit of dirty business."

Hatch felt the sting of his words. The promise she'd broken would be the undoing of an innocent woman and her children. She shifted her attention to Hurley. "I know there was a time before all this. A time where being a Marine mattered to you. Whatever brought you to the here and now doesn't have to hold you on this path."

"Head games don't work. Not at this point. Not with me." Hurley's expression remained unchanged. "The whys and hows mean nothing. Believe me, Hatch, there's a point of no return everyone can reach. And I crossed it the moment I knocked Ryker out of that chopper."

"Enough chit-chat. We've got a bird to catch." Granger flicked his hand toward Hatch as if shoeing a fly. "Get to steppin'. That way."

Hatch turned and began walking to the far corner of the building. With her back to the two men, she tried to gauge distance in the footfalls. Adding in the fact she no longer had a visual only served to increase the odds of failure. Hatch continued to hold out for her opportunity. Now was not it.

They rounded the corner. An SUV was parked under the shadow of the building, further shrouded by overgrown shrubbery. As the footsteps fell silent, Hatch heard the muffled anguish coming from the rear of the vehicle.

"Turn around," Granger commanded.

Hatch faced the two men. Hurley kept his distance, his gun still trained on her. Granger tossed over plastic zip tie cuffs, and she caught them in midair.

"Put 'em on."

She slipped her hands through the loops and tugged at the ends, ratcheting them down on her wrists. Hatch tried to leave some wiggle room, but neither of the men standing before her were amateurs. Granger stepped forward as Hurley stepped off to the right, maintaining his target.

Granger gave a quick tug on each end, tightening the restraints against her skin.

The rear door lifted, releasing the muffled anguish of the woman trapped inside. Granger shoved Hatch's shoulder, pushing her forward toward the backend of the SUV. She locked eyes with Santiago.

The detective was bound in a similar fashion. The only difference was that her mouth was covered in a strip of gray duct tape.

Another shove from behind sent Hatch forward into the rear bumper. Santiago muffled through her gag as a hand reached around Hatch's mouth, the chloroform's intended effects kicking in instantly. Hatch fell into the cargo area and on top of Santiago. Hands grabbed her legs and shoved them further into the small compartment. A moment later, the door lowered, sealing them inside. Her eyes fighting to stay open, the dizzying blow slowly winning the battle.

The engine roared to life. Hatch jostled as the vehicle rumbled across the lot. The turbulence subsided as the road smoothed. Where it would take them was uncertain. She prepared her mind for whatever was coming.

As the world around her fell out of focus, one thing became clear. Regardless of the odds, Hatch refused to lie down and die. If it was her time to face the reaper, she'd stand toe to toe and give him the fight of her life.

# THIRTY-SEVEN

HATCH'S EYES FLUTTERED OPEN, HER VISION HAZY AND UNFOCUSED AS SHE struggled to regain her bearings. Her chin was pressed against her chest, a result of her awkward position while unconscious. As she forced herself to sit up, her neck protested, aching from the strain of supporting her head's weight during the unintended slumber.

Something was off. Hatch had taken many blows to the head throughout her life, the disorientation, fogginess of thought, and lapse in time led her to conclude they'd drugged her after knocking her out. The rumble of the SUV had changed. Another sound replaced it, a familiar one, but in her hazy return to consciousness, it was just out of grasp. A rush of air blew her hair back, and Hatch's eyes came into focus.

The thunderous roar of helicopter rotors permeated the air above her, drowning out any other sounds. She was airborne. Hatch scanned the ground below, only to find a deeper darkness than the stormy sky stretching out above. The moon hid behind the clouds as the aircraft navigated the endless gulf.

Disoriented, she had no true accounting for time. Based on the distance from where Granger had shown his true colors, to the base they'd lifted off, Hatch calculated she'd been out for at least thirty minutes, probably longer.

The next thought went to Sophia. Granger had alluded to his intention. She hoped he hadn't yet made good on it. The only thing Hatch could do was deal with the problem at hand. She looked to her left and saw Santiago strapped into her chair. Two seats separated Hatch from the detective.

Santiago caught sight of Hatch's movement. The two locked eyes. She could read the concern in Santiago's expression. Hatch gave a slow, reassuring nod before shifting in her seat to scan the remainder of the helicopter's interior.

Granger was in the pilot's seat with Hurley taking up the co-pilot's position. Both men had on helmets and were communicating via the internal mic system. Hatch could not make out what they were saying over the thrumming of the rotor blades and the rushing wind flooding through the open doors on either side of the passenger compartment.

The two seemed not to notice Hatch's alertness. Under the shift in circumstance, she began recalculating her odds. The percentages began shifting, albeit only slightly, in her favor.

Hatch's wrists remained bound. The seat's harness locked her in place. She was, however, able to move her hands along the outside of her pants to her thigh. It took only a moment to find what she was looking for.

They hadn't taken the time to remove her cellphone. A mistake she planned to capitalize on. Hatch wriggled her fingertips under the lap harness and clawed at the phone until she pulled it through.

Hatch shot a glance at Hurley. He remained oblivious to her movement and focused his gaze on the horizon. She made quick work of scrolling through her contacts. Finding Tracy, she opted for a text. She used one finger to tap out her message. It was short and to the point.

*Ganger and Hurley bad guys. Trapped on helicopter over the gulf. Santiago with me. Sophia in danger. Hit squad coming for her. Send help.*

She hit send, slipping the phone back into the recesses of her pocket and hoping the message was received and enough time remained on the clock to save Sophia. The survival of Hatch and Santiago rested squarely on her shoulders.

Hatch twisted her hands upward and undid the latches of her harness.

She did her best to keep them in place to maintain the illusion that she was still strapped into her seat. She shot a glance at Santiago and gave a wink of encouragement. The detective was completely out of her element and frozen with fear, as evident in the expression on her face. Hatch accepted the fact she'd be taking on the threat alone.

She dropped her chin, letting her head bobble loosely to the helicopter's gyrations, maintaining the illusion of her unconscious state. She closed her eyes, leaving only slits from which to see. In her periphery, Hatch saw Hurley undo his harness straps and rise from his seat. He navigated his way to the passenger compartment. The gun was no longer in his hand, now tucked into a drop-down holster on his right leg.

Hurley kept careful watch on Hatch as he approached. Once in the passenger area, he stood erect and kept balance by holding onto the thick, braided rope that hung from the metal gantry arm and piled into a bulky coil at his boot. A snarl formed on his face as he surveyed the two women seated before him.

"Wake up, buttercup," Hurley boomed.

Hatch continued her ruse, bobbing her head and acting as though his words were slowly working to wake her. She lifted her gaze to the imposing man towering above her.

"Sorry it had to come to this." Hurley's face conveyed the truth behind the words.

"It didn't have to." Hatch did her best to carry her voice above the noise.

"It'll all be over soon." Hurley took a step forward. The helicopter shuddered in the turbulent air, causing him to stagger. His grip on the rope halted him from falling headfirst into Hatch.

She watched his eyes widen at the realization her harness was no longer secured. His right hand still clutched the rope, interfering with his ability to retrieve his sidearm.

In the split second it took for Hatch to re-evaluate, she knew the opportunity was now. The old familiarity of the battle at hand returned. Tempered by reason. Driven by purpose. Hatch sprang into action.

As the helicopter's nose tilted skyward to adjust to volatile air, Hurley's unbalanced stance betrayed him, sending him stumbling sideways. Santiago's composure returned. Seeing the Marine stagger her way, she kicked out her leg. Santiago's shin connected with the outside of Hurley's knee.

He released the rope as he fell against the unforgiving metal wall dividing the compartment from the helicopter's tail section. Hurley remained stunned for the briefest of seconds. Gnashed teeth and fiery eyes bore down on Hatch, disregarding Santiago for the moment while he focused his attention on the biggest threat.

His hand swept down toward the pistol on his thigh. The distance between them was short enough to cross, but the unpredictable shifting of the aircraft would make it difficult before he could draw the gun. Hatch saw an alternative and made her move.

As the web of Hurley's hand slammed into the tang of the Glock, Hatch reached to her left. In one swift move, she released the nearby fire extinguisher. If this were the old west, tumbleweed would have drifted across their path.

In a draw down between pistol and extinguisher, the split second of action versus reaction prevailed. Hatch released the retaining pin and engaged the trigger mechanism, releasing a burst of white.

Hurley, just a hair behind, took the full blast in his face. He brought his pistol up and fired blindly at where Hatch had been standing only moments before.

His rounds clanged into the metal fuselage, ricocheting the lead in all directions. Hatch changed positions as soon as she sprayed the canister, diving to her left and tucking low behind the opposite side row of bench seats.

The flex cuffs bit down into the flesh at her wrists, the hard plastic limiting her range of motion and reducing her options for counterattack. She thought of the lesson she'd taught Jake before leaving Hawk's Landing about how anything could be a weapon in the right hands. She felt the metal cylinder in her clutch. Hatch decided to put her wisdom to the test.

Hurley cleared his eyes, wiping away white froth from his face with his left forearm while he swung the gun in a desperate search for his attacker. Granger twisted in his seat. He called out something inaudible to Hurley, likely a warning.

Hatch was already moving. The empty canister became a baton in her hands. She gripped it at the nozzle end and swung hard. The metal collided with Hurley's extended forearm. The impact was devastating, shattering the bone above the wrist. The gun dropped from his grip and slid along the floor. Santiago trapped it under her foot.

Hurley gripped his broken arm, clutching it against his chest. His eyes wild with rage, he sidestepped his way back toward the cockpit, navigating the bench in an effort to close the gap on Hatch. He may have been injured, but she could see he was by no means out of the fight.

Just as he reached the divide between the two rows of seats, the helicopter rolled to its side. Hatch looked toward Granger and understood why. One of Hurley's bullets had found its mark. Blood leaked from the side of his neck. One hand fought to control the stick while the other worked to slow the bleeding, doing an ineffective job at both.

The roll threw Hurley backward toward the open door behind him. He released his injured arm in a desperate attempt to grab hold of the rope with his left. His fingertips grazed the coarse fibers but failed to gain purchase.

As he fell out of the cabin, Hurley locked eyes with Hatch. The anger was gone. Hatch saw a peace wash over him. Death had been a longtime companion for the decorated Marine. And he seemed to welcome its embrace.

Then he was gone. Dark air consumed him. The fall, several hundred feet, would turn the water to concrete. Hatch calculated the probability of survival to be zero.

She immediately turned her attention to Granger. Scooping up the gun Santiago had secured under her foot, Hatch pointed it in the direction of the dirty NCIS agent.

With the gun trained on him, Hatch navigated her way to the cockpit and assumed the seat once held by Hurley. Granger shifted his gaze from the gun to meet the eyes of the woman holding it. His face was paler than normal, the blood loss taking its toll.

Hatch held the gun steady, the flex cuffs forcing her to do so with both hands. "Time to RTB!" Hatch shouted over the noise.

Granger looked to be considering the option of returning to base or ditching into the ocean. Hatch was glad to see self-preservation triumph.

Hatch looked out to see the lights of the naval air station in the distance ahead. With the current threat eliminated, her mind shifted to Sophia and her children.

# THIRTY-EIGHT

HATCH MAINTAINED A FIRM GRIP ON HER WEAPON, KEEPING IT POINTED AT Granger as they made their final descent. Red and blue strobe lights bounced off the buildings surrounding the tarmac. As they drew closer, Hatch could see Marine MPs standing at the ready.

Granger was fighting unconsciousness. Santiago delivered a slap to the side of his head to keep him alert enough to bring this roller coaster ride to an end.

Santiago had taken up a rear facing seat behind Granger. She'd managed to cut the plastic, separating the cuffs. She'd taken the gun and kept it pointed at Granger while Hatch cut herself free. The plastic bracelets bit into her skin, but at least she now had freedom of movement.

Granger looked at the circus below. His lips drew up in a wicked smile. "I radioed ahead. Looks like you've got yourself a welcoming party when we land."

Hatch edged toward him, bringing the end of the barrel closer to the side of his head. "I'm pretty sure they'll see things more clearly once we're on the ground."

Granger coughed blood. "You killed a Marine First Sergeant. Not sure how they do things in the Army, but those men and women down there are gonna be looking for that pound of flesh."

"They'll get it. Just not from me." Hatch looked at the former Marine helicopter pilot turned NCIS agent turned criminal. His vitals appeared to be touch and go. She put the odds at fifty-fifty he'd survive the wound. The probability was on a downward slide. "Why'd you do it? It couldn't have just been for the money."

"Need a better reason?" His eyes grew more vacant.

"Doesn't add up." Hatch gauged the dying man's expressionless face. "Money's usually not a motivator. Not for those who serve. If it was, we'd probably pick a different line of work."

Granger's eyes glossed over. "Drugs took my son's life. I failed to protect him."

"And you decided to steal them as a way of retribution?"

"No. Well, I guess. Figured hitting them in the wallet was a way I could do the most damage." Granger shrugged. The movement of his shoulder caused him to wince. "If I bankrupted enough of them, they'd die off."

"But you couldn't do it alone?" Hatch asked.

"No. Way too dangerous. Probably wouldn't have made it through the first door."

"And that's where Hurley and his men came in?" Santiago chimed in.

Granger gave a slow nod. "Sold it as a way of taking back the streets from thugs just as bad, if not worse, than some of the shitbirds we faced off with in the sandbox. Easy sell, really."

"I guess the money didn't hurt, either?" Santiago asked. "If my numbers are right, you and Hurley's team cleared nearly five hundred thousand since you started."

"More like six, but who's counting?" Granger was ghost-white now. His hands shook as he fought to maintain his grip on the stick. "Never meant for it to get bloody. Hurley and his guys were top tier. Figured we'd overwhelm the enemy. Shock and awe style."

"There's always a percentage of risk."

"Guess we didn't weight it properly." Blood frothed from the corners of his mouth as he spoke. "Can't take it back now."

"You put an innocent woman and her children in the crosshairs to cover your ass," Santiago growled.

The stalwart detective looked as though she were going to pounce. Hatch reached out a hand and placed it on her shoulder to settle her.

"Survival is an instinct. People like us..." He canted his head in the direction of Hatch and continued, "we don't even recognize when it kicks in. Second nature, I guess."

Hatch understood the point he was trying to make. She didn't agree with its application to this circumstance.

"War's an ugly thing."

"This isn't war," Santiago countered.

"Everything is. Problem is people don't recognize it." Granger's eyes started to close. He jolted awake, tugging the stick, causing the helicopter to dip. Hatch put her hand over his and assisted in guiding it. The craft stabilized. He gave her a grateful look. "You do though. You're no sheep. I know a wolf when I see one."

Hatch offered nothing in return. She focused on the approaching concrete of the tarmac. Seeing the speed of their approach, she gave a warning shout to Santiago, then braced for impact.

The UH-1Y Venom slammed into the ground. It hit at an awkward angle with the right skid making contact first. The off-balanced landing nearly sent the craft spiraling out of control. Granger toggled the stick with the last bit of lifeforce left in his withering body. It was just enough to avoid catastrophe. The left skid touched down. The rotors slowed, and the helicopter came to rest.

Hatch watched as the MPs made a tactical approach, edging forward with their duty weapons drawn, while several others provided overwatch with long guns. Their verbal commands were covered by the whir of the engine as it wound down. She looked over at Granger. His chin slumped against his chest. His hand no longer covered the gunshot wound. The blood continued to flow but had slowed to a trickle. The seat harness was the only thing keeping his body from collapsing forward onto the center console.

She lowered the gun to her lap. Hatch reached out along the side of Granger's neck. She slid two fingers along the carotid. No pulse. She retracted her hand and wiped the blood from her fingers onto her pant leg. Hatch turned to Santiago and shook her head.

"Not the closure I'd hoped for," Santiago said.

"Beats the alternative."

Hatch set the pistol down on the instrument panel and raised her hands in surrender. Santiago followed suit. The MPs converged. They appeared alongside the open side doors. Seeing Granger's condition, they dropped their weapons to a low, ready position.

"Ms. Hatch, Detective Santiago, lower your weapons." An MP wearing the rank of Master Sergeant spoke calmly and clearly, holstering his weapon as he stepped forward. "We received word from a Jordan Tracy. He advised us on the situation." He dipped his head inside the cabin, his eyes came to rest on Granger. "Glad to see you're both okay."

Hatch and Santiago were escorted from the helicopter to a waiting ambulance. Two Marines entered to further inspect Granger. They called out from inside, notifying the supervisor of his status.

The plastic bracelets were cut free by the medics. Both Hatch and Santiago worked the circulation back into their hands, rubbing gingerly at the abrasions left behind by their captors. They were evaluated for injury. The medic who inspected Hatch's head wound recommended she go to the hospital for further treatment. She declined.

They sat on the bumper of the ambulance. The ensuing chaos died down, and Hatch and her detective counterpart drifted into the backdrop while the scene was processed. She pulled her cell from her pocket and dialed Tracy.

He answered before the first ring ended. "Hatch?"

"Alive and kicking." She shifted tone. "Tell me you got my message in time to do something about Sophia?"

"Banyan was already on the ground when I got your message. He placed a call to the state police. They were able to intercept Brunson, Li, and Woodrow."

Hatch let out an exhale. The pang of anxiety she'd held onto since realizing her mistake in trusting Granger with Sophia's whereabouts was finally released. She felt a calm wash over her, a feeling foreign to Hatch in the months since Cruise's death.

"They're okay, then?"

"They are. Thanks to you."

Hatch felt like elaborating on the fallacy of his statement but decided to hold off and let the dust settle a bit before rehashing her mistake. "Where are they now?"

"State police were keeping them safe until we were able to ensure the other threats had been addressed. Then she'll be heading home."

"Sounds like she's in the clear." Hatch turned to the helicopter as several Marines worked to extricate the body of Agent Beau Granger.

"I just got off the phone with Banyan. He's wrapping up things with state police right now. Once they've cleared you, why don't you head back to your motel and get some rest? Banyan will be by in the morning to pick you up."

"Pick me up? What for?" Hatch thought of her family, and the promise she'd made to return as soon as possible. "I thought I'd stick around for a day or so before heading back home."

"I'm going to need you back here," Tracy said, "and based on what just transpired, it sounds to me like you're ready."

"Fair enough." Before she hung up, Hatch said, "But don't have him pick me up at the motel. There's a diner down the road. I'll be there." She then relayed the name and address of the diner to Tracy and ended the call.

Santiago was looking over at her. She held an ice pack on the back of her neck. "Leaving so soon?"

"Duty calls." Hatch shrugged, her mind on her niece and nephew.

Santiago shifted her gaze to the helicopter where they'd narrowly escaped death. "You saved my life."

"I think we're even on that one. Never would've been able to maintain the advantage had it not been for you." Hatch placed a hand on Santiago's shoulder. "You're one hell of a cop. Glad to see there're people like you still holding the line."

Santiago smiled but didn't accept the compliment. "What's next for you?"

"Wish I knew. My path is dimly lit. And it usually takes until I'm one step away before I can see where the next one will land me."

"Well, if it ever brings you back this way, know that you've got someone in your corner."

"Santiago?" A man with thinning hair and glasses wearing slacks and a blue police windbreaker called out as he hustled across the tarmac in the direction of the ambulances.

"Captain." Santiago pushed off the bumper and stood.

Hatch remained in the background and watched the exchange. Her captain showed no anger in his expression. All Hatch saw was concern.

"Before you say a thing, all I want to know is, are you okay?"

"Right as rain." Santiago set the ice pack down on the bumper where she'd just been sitting. She shifted uneasily. "Should I plan on packing up my desk?"

Captain Parnell shook his head. "On the contrary. We've been brought up to speed on everything." Parnell's voice lowered, and his shoulders drooped slightly. "I should've listened to you. Should've had your back. We all should've."

"I wasn't right about everything." Santiago looked past Parnell to the black bag on the tarmac where Granger's body was now enclosed.

"Maybe. But you were spot on when it came to your assessment of Malcolm's abilities as a detective." His lips drew into a smile. "He dropped the ball on this case in more ways than one. And it almost cost multiple innocent lives."

"Just glad it didn't come to that."

"You're reinstated. Suspension lifted, starting immediatcly." Parnell looked toward the MPs huddled by a command vehicle. "I'll make sure things are cleared up here so you can get home to your daughter."

"Thanks."

"Oh, and Santiago," Parnell said. "How'd you like a position working Homicide?"

"Not sure I'd jive with the lead detective." Santiago gave a roll of her eyes.

"That'd be you." Parnell began walking away. "Malcolm's under review. Doesn't look like he'll be able to bullshit his way out of this one. Best case scenario, he'll be pushing a black and white until retirement."

Santiago grinned tiredly at her superior. "I'll see you in the morning."

"Not tomorrow. You take that time with your family." He then cast a glance over his shoulder. "That was some damn fine policework."

"Looks like we're both getting back on track," Hatch said to Santiago as Parnell disappeared into a crowd of MPs.

"Appears so."

Hatch lifted herself off the backend of the ambulance and stood shoulder to shoulder with Santiago as they took in the finality of the scene before them. Maybe Tracy should become a weatherman. His predication about the shitstorm had been spot on.

Her time in Panama City was coming to an end. But Hatch still needed closure on a couple of things before moving on. She planned on ticking one of those off her list before heading to the motel.

# THIRTY-NINE

HATCH AND SANTIAGO HAD BEEN TRANSPORTED BACK TO THEIR RESPECTIVE vehicles that had been left parked behind the abandoned warehouse. She'd spent a couple minutes saying goodbye to the detective before they went their separate ways. Santiago headed for home. Hatch headed to see Renee.

The picturesque neighborhood was cast in the dark shadow of night. Hatch couldn't help feeling as though an added darkness hung over the Ryker residence. She parked out front. It was late, but through the light cascading out of the front window, Hatch could see Renee hunched over her kitchen table.

Hatch made the walk up to the door. Only days before, the path had been lined by Marines, paying their respects for the fallen. So much had changed since then. Hatch knew it would never be the same for any of them, most of all for the wife and daughter left to pick up the pieces.

She stood at the front door, breathing in the quiet. Hatch gave a gentle knock, hoping it was loud enough for Renee to hear, but not so much as to wake her young daughter.

Light footsteps sounded on the other side. A moment later, the door opened. Renee's puffy red eyes stared up at Hatch. The widow stepped forward into the thick warm air and pulled Hatch into a tight embrace.

The two remained locked together for several moments before separating. Renee stepped back and invited Hatch inside.

"Can I get you some tea, maybe a cup of coffee?" Renee asked.

"No need to trouble yourself."

"No trouble at all. I've got a pot already brewed." Renee stepped over to the kitchen counter. "I know it's supposed to be bad to drink coffee before bed. But never had much of an effect on me."

"Same here." Hatch accepted the cup.

She then followed Renee over to the table. Cardboard boxes were on the floor, and photographs were scattered across the round tabletop. Her eyes scanned the images, cataloging a career of military service and the family that had grown up around it.

Renee pushed a loose pile away, clearing a space for Hatch to rest her mug. "Sorry for the mess. I'm trying to organize some photos for the service. I don't even know where to begin."

Hatch could hear the pain in her voice. "It's never easy to sum up the measure of a person's life. Not sure it's even possible." Hatch thought of the losses she'd faced over the years. The mental imagery constantly reshuffled, calling forward the memories as needed. Her father had come to her many times over the years since his passing. His advice had served to save her life on several occasions. Priceless wisdom, perpetually engrained in Hatch's mind.

"I saw the news." Renee's voice was a whisper. "I still can't believe it. My husband … he was a part of all that."

"I think he thought he was doing some good. At least, I'd like to think it started that way." Hatch rested a hand on Renee's. She felt a tremble beneath her palm. "Sometimes good intentions can lead us down the wrong path. And with it, the fallout of unintended consequences. The risks you took in bringing to light the connection to Hurley's team enabled me to fit the pieces of the puzzle together. What you did helped save the life of a mother and her two young boys."

"Thank you for that." Renee kept her head down, her eyes sweeping to the moments in time reflected beneath the glossy coating. "Not sure the rest of the world will see it that way. Not sure we'll be able to stay. Too much pain. Don't think I could face the neighbors."

"I get it. I've spent the majority of my life running from my past," Hatch said.

"Did it work?"

"I'm still running, so I haven't found out yet." Hatch offered a smile in a weak attempt at lifting the mood, knowing it was unlikely anything could.

"The news didn't go into detail. But it sounds like more tragedy resulted from whatever this was."

"It's over now."

Renee's body shook. No tears fell. Hatch could see her friend's widower was empty.

"I found something after you left. I had intended on showing it to you. Not sure it matters now." Renee slipped her hand out from under Hatch's and began sifting through the pictures.

Hatch watched as Renee pushed piles aside until she came to an 8x10. She held it in front of her, staring at it briefly before handing it over. The image captured was of Ryker and several members of his fellow Marines. They wore tattered, dust-covered fatigues. Each man in the staggered line posed, some holding their weapons. Hatch recognized the photo, commonplace among servicemembers on deployment. A way of capturing the people in the foxhole who stood alongside each other in front of death's door.

Her eyes moved across the picture, capturing the image of seven combat hardened Marines standing in front of a helicopter. The dry dirt at their feet and shadowed mountains in the distance placed the photo somewhere in the Afghan countryside. A couple of days prior, aside from Ryker, none of the other faces would've held any meaning. Seeing them now, Hatch recognized them all.

Ryker was on the far right. Scribbled in black ink underneath him was the word *Striker*. To his immediate left was Roger Kastner, *Flask* written in the same manner. Moving down the line, the shortest of the Marines in the group, stood Mark Li, or *Swift*. Next to him was James Woodrow, *Woody*. The muscle-bound Greg Brunson, the Marine Staff Sergeant who first introduced himself to Hatch when she'd arrived, stood with his arms folded, the word *Colt* written over the man's thick forearms.

Standing several inches above the rest was First Sergeant Calvin

Hurley. Seeing him there with his hands on his hips and his chest puffed out, Hatch felt the pride his image conveyed. She tried to replace the one in her head, and the look in his eyes just before he disappeared into the blackness. She couldn't, resigning herself to the fact that the Marine in the picture died the moment he'd killed the two men in that apartment, maybe before. Whatever was left would be unrecognizable to those who knew him on the battlefield. *Cain* was written below. Ryker's death proved his nickname was true the moment Hurley took the life of a brother-in-arms.

But it was the last man in line, the one standing a foot or so away from Hurley. He was a tall, thin Marine wearing a flight suit. His hair was in the high and tight typical of a Marine, unlike the long unkempt look he took upon leaving his time in service. Scribbled beneath Beau Granger's midline was his callsign. *Gypsy.*

"I used to love that photograph." Renee looked away. "Now, I can't stand to look at it."

"That's the thing with pictures. You don't have to." Hatch tucked it under the pile, burying it deep.

"I guess you're right. I'm just thinking of my daughter. The questions she'll have as she gets older. And the answers I won't know how to give."

"Those answers will come when you need them." Hatch looked at the refrigerator and the picture stuck to it by a magnet. The crayon image of Ryker, captured from the mind of his daughter. The image she'd likely hold on to for years to come, possibly for the rest of her life. "How you keep your memories is up to you. And your daughter will know him through the stories you tell. In time, the taint of recent events will fade. You'll remember the things that mattered, the feelings you had, and you'll be able to call them forward."

Renee's well had replenished, and tears began to stream down her face. She made a lazy attempt to wipe them away. "Maybe you should be a therapist." She choked out a laugh that came out more like a cough.

Hatch thought of the therapy she'd been applying since leaving the service. The code her father imbued in her those many years ago. The only thing that satisfied her quest for salvation. *Help good people and punish those who hurt them.* The path was a long and winding one, but she was now convinced if she walked it long enough, it would lead her to the peace envisioned in her mind's eye. Hatch exhaled and released the thought, knowing it was still a journey away.

Renee collected herself, ebbing the flow of tears and letting out a gentle sigh. "Will you be attending the funeral?"

"I don't think so." Hatch avoided looking into her eyes, feeling the disappointment flooding the room around her. "I've got somewhere I need to be."

"I'm sorry to hear that." Renee wiped her nose with a tissue. "I know if you're being called away, it must be important."

Hatch didn't elaborate, offering a nod instead.

"Thank you for what you've done. Regardless of what happens next, I know that if Jeff were alive, he would've backed you one hundred percent."

"I'd like to believe that too." Hatch stood. "I'll remember him the way I always have, as a soldier and friend."

Renee stood and walked Hatch to the door. They embraced once more, a heartfelt exchange that left Hatch more drained than the battle she'd just waged.

Feeling the exhaustion sweep over her as she drove away, Hatch thought of the clean linen sheets awaiting her at the motel. A well-deserved night of sleep and a hearty breakfast the following morning should do the trick in resetting her mind for the path ahead.

# FORTY

Hatch woke early, just before the sun began its climb. She ran the city sprawl, taking in the sleeping neighborhoods as she pounded the pavement. The humidity made the ground slick as she made her way toward the gulf. The gentle breeze coming off the water felt cool against her sweat-soaked skin. Hatch continued along the jogging path for another mile or so before coming to a bench set a few feet off the trail near the water's edge.

She slowed and continued to shuffle her feet, running in place. Hatch decided to take a moment to stretch her muscles. The run served the purpose of both clearing her head and circulating the lactic acid built up from her physical exertion in overpowering Hurley during their life and death struggle the night before. Hatch pressed her hands against the backing of the bench and worked her hamstrings, alternating legs, until both felt loose.

The sound of the lapping water against the shore called to her. After Cruise's death, Hatch spent some time in the Pacific Northwest trying to make sense of it all. The ocean, the final resting place for the man she'd loved but failed to commit to, had called him home. Hearing it now brought an image of his face to mind. Since that tragic night, when Cruise had put his life before Hatch and others, she could only conjure the last time she saw him. It haunted her.

But here, in the serenity of the calm water glittering under the Florida sunrise, she began to call forward the Cruise from before. Hatch could see the cobalt blue of his eyes. In the salty air swirling around her, she smelled the all-too familiar musk of the former SEAL who seemed to carry the ocean breeze wherever he roamed.

Hatch slipped off her shoes and socks, setting them beside the bench. She walked forward on the cool patch of grass and down to the sandy lip connecting the land to the sea. Her toes felt the tingle as the ripples flowed over them.

Two steps forward and the waterline reached the bottom of her knees. The cold felt good against her warm leg muscles. Hatch felt the tremble in her chest. It resonated throughout her body. Standing there, alone except for the endless sea, Hatch opened herself to the pain she'd locked away.

She couldn't remember the last time she'd allowed herself to give into emotion, to truly let go. "I'm sorry." The words meant only for the ocean and the man who would always be a part of it. It was the code that opened the door to the floodgates. Tears streamed down her face, adding Hatch's salty brine to the mix.

Hatch didn't feel the passage of time, only the long-overdue release. When she'd emptied her heart into the ocean, Hatch walked back to the bench. She allowed the breeze to dry both the water from her legs and the tears from her eyes. Slipping her socks and sneakers back on, Hatch began her trek back to the motel. Each footfall felt lighter than the one before. The burden she'd been shouldering wasn't gone, but its load had been reduced. She hoped the same would prove true for Renee and her daughter.

AFTER A QUICK SHOWER and an even quicker packing job, Hatch was ready to leave. She stopped into the office to settle her tab with Oak. The old fan still rattled in its ineffective battle to vanquish the heat from the room. She didn't need to tag the bell. Oak was seated in a wooden swivel chair behind the desk, reading the local paper.

He looked up at Hatch with a smile on his face. "Good to see you this fine mornin', Hatch. And how did you sleep?"

"Better than I've slept in a long time." Hatch reached into her pocket and placed the cash on the table. "I think that settles us."

Oak looked saddened by the news. "Leavin' so soon?"

"My life doesn't lend itself to staying in one place for too long."

"It's a shame. If you don't lay your roots, you're never gonna grow."

"Someday." Hatch hoped her words would prove true.

"Where to next?"

Hatch shrugged. "I guess I'll know when I get there. I'm sure it'll be between somewhere and nowhere."

"How's that?"

"Just something we used to say in my previous life."

Oak nodded. His kind eyes held the wisdom of his years, much like the tree he was nicknamed after. "I hope the life you want, the one you deserve, finds you well."

Hatch smiled and exited the office. Oak stood in the doorway and watched her go.

THE DRIVE to the diner took no time at all. Hatch parked the rental car in front and walked inside. She was happy to see that after calling Sophia earlier this morning, she'd been able to get here on short notice.

Hatch walked inside and approached the booth where Sophia sat alongside her two children. The boys were already working their way through a stack of pancakes, syrup dripping down their chins as they shoveled the food into their mouths.

Sophia was giving a quick lesson on manners. She looked up at Hatch. A smile stretched across her face. "Boys will be boys."

"Can't blame them. The food here's worth inhaling." Hatch slipped onto the worn leather seat of the booth across from Sophia. "I'm glad to see you and your children are safe."

"Wouldn't have been, if it wasn't for you."

"About that ... I'm sorry. I broke my promise." Hatch turned the coffee mug right side up on the small plate. "I told the wrong person your whereabouts."

Sophia waved a hand. "Don't you go putting any blame on yourself. You did what you thought was right. I know that. I also know that if it wasn't for you, I'd be looking over my shoulder for the rest of my life."

Hatch knew what that felt like. She didn't wish it upon anyone, especially for the kindhearted mother sitting across from her.

"Besides, today's a day of celebration." Sophia rubbed the top of her youngest boy's head, seated closest to her.

Louise, Sophia's niece and the person responsible for getting Hatch involved, walked over with a smile matching that of her aunt's.

"Today, my husband comes home." Sophia spoke with pride, the same pride she'd seen among families of deployed service members upon their return. "I have faith it will be a new beginning for all of us."

"It'll sure be nice to have him around here," Louise said. "My father'd be real proud."

"I'm sure he would." Hatch turned her gaze to Sophia. "You're one of the strongest people I've met. Your boys are lucky to have you."

Sophia's eyes glossed over. "Means a lot coming from someone like you. I don't have the words for what you've done for me and my family."

"Seeing you here, together like this, is all the thanks I need." Hatch caught sight of a man outside the diner window standing near her car. Ed Banyan leaned against the PT Cruiser's hood. His arms folded. He smiled at her. She gave him a nod in return.

"Someone here to see you?" Sophia asked. "Have him come on in. Plenty of room."

"Wish there was time." Hatch took one last mental picture of the family before her, filing it away and knowing a time would come when she'd need to draw strength from this moment.

Hatch stood, and Sophia did so as well. She pulled Hatch into a bear hug. The warmth of her embrace felt good, and Hatch soaked it in. Like a comforting meal, she drew in strength for the road ahead. They separated, and Hatch made her way toward the door.

Louise rushed up behind her. "Hold up. I can't have you leave without some of our turtle pie."

Hatch accepted the boxed pie and reached for her wallet.

Louise shook her head. "Don't you dare. I only wish there was more I could give you for what you did for my aunt, for my family."

"This is more than enough. Thank you."

"You take care of yourself out there. The world's a dangerous place."

Hatch smiled. "I'll keep that in mind."

She waved one last time to Louise and Sophia, then pushed her way through the diner's door. Banyan hadn't moved since Hatch had spotted him from the window.

"You kick ass *and* eat pie." Banyan pushed off the car and gave Hatch a toothy grin. "I see nothing's changed. I should tell Tracy you work for food. It'd save the company some good money."

Hatch laughed and opened the door to the rental. "Follow me to the airport. Got to drop it off."

"Already taken care of. Just leave the keys in the glovebox. Someone will be by to pick it up." Banyan gestured toward a navy-blue Jeep. "I'll take the pie. You grab your stuff."

"And whoever said chivalry is dead." Hatch smirked and handed off the pie.

As they drove away from the diner, Hatch pulled out her cellphone. She dialed the number and a woman's voice answered.

"Hello, Econo Rentals, this Martha speaking. How may I help you?"

"Hi, Martha. It's Rachel Hatch."

"Hey there. Someone already arranged to have your car turned in." Martha sounded disappointed. "You know you still have that two-hundred-dollar cash deposit here."

"It's one of the reasons I was calling."

"I was also hoping to get to see you before you left." Her voice was lower. Her hand cupping the receiver muffled her words. "Been thinking about our conversation. I'm tired of taking crap from my manager. As of the end of the day today, I'll be officially done."

"What's next?"

"I've got a couple things lined up. For the first time in a long time, I'm excited about my future." Martha's voice perked up.

"Glad to hear it. And about that security deposit. It's yours to keep."

"Oh, you don't have to do that. I can't—"

"Consider it seed money. I hope it helps you until you get your footing."

"Girl power, right?"

"Absolutely." Hatch tapped the phone off. The smile on her face continued after the call had ended. She looked at Banyan behind the wheel. "What's the situation? Tracy didn't tell me much."

"Still working on the details. We'll get a full workup once we're on site." Banyan kept his eyes on the stop-and-go traffic. "Tracy decided it's a good idea for you to have a callsign."

"They've never stuck." Hatch thought of the few times she'd been given one. Her last name was the only calling card capable of enduring the tests of time. She then thought of the photograph and the battle branded names of the Marines she'd faced off against.

"I don't think it's up for debate."

"Well, what is it?"

"Hawk."

Hatch thought about it for a moment and followed with a slow nod of consideration.

"Figured you might like it, seeing as how you're from Hawk's Landing."

"It works for me."

Hatch might not be able to go home yet, but at least her new callsign enabled her, in some small way, to carry a small piece of it forward with her. Wherever the path may lead.

---

**Rachel Hatch will return in *Sidewinder*.**

In a shadowy world where covert operations and secret agendas rule, a top-tier team of private contractors vanishes. They leave behind a chilling trail of breadcrumbs that point to a cache of advanced, portable missiles gone rogue.

Rachel Hatch, a warrior with a steel spine and a heart of grit, is called upon to find the lost operatives. As she peels back layers of deception, she realizes that the stakes are far higher than anyone could have guessed. Lives hang precariously in the balance, and a malevolent organization emerges from the shadows, hungry for the lethal firepower…

**Pre-order your copy of Sidewinder now:**
https://www.amazon.com/gp/product/B0C4BBSYKF

Join the LT Ryan reader family & receive a free copy of the Rachel Hatch story, *Fractured*. Click the link below to get started:
https://ltryan.com/rachel-hatch-newsletter-signup-1

# THE RACHEL HATCH SERIES

Drift

Downburst

Fever Burn

Smoke Signal

Firewalk

Whitewater

Aftershock

Whirlwind

Tsunami

Fastrope

Sidewinder (Pre-Order now)

## RACHEL HATCH SHORT STORIES

Fractured

Proving Ground

The Gauntlet

# ALSO BY L.T. RYAN

**Find All of L.T. Ryan's Books on Amazon Today!**

## The Jack Noble Series

*The Recruit (free)*

*The First Deception (Prequel 1)*

*Noble Beginnings*

*A Deadly Distance*

*Ripple Effect (Bear Logan)*

*Thin Line*

*Noble Intentions*

*When Dead in Greece*

*Noble Retribution*

*Noble Betrayal*

*Never Go Home*

*Beyond Betrayal (Clarissa Abbot)*

*Noble Judgment*

*Never Cry Mercy*

*Deadline*

*End Game*

*Noble Ultimatum*

*Noble Legend (2022)*

## **Bear Logan Series**

*Ripple Effect*

*Blowback*

*Take Down*

*Deep State*

## **Bear & Mandy Logan Series**

*Close to Home*

*Under the Surface*

*The Last Stop*

*Over the Edge (Coming Soon)*

## **Rachel Hatch Series**

*Drift*

*Downburst*

*Fever Burn*

*Smoke Signal*

*Firewalk*

*Whitewater*

*Aftershock*

*Whirlwind*

*Tsunami*

*Fastrope*

*Sidewinder (Pre-Order Now)*

## Mitch Tanner Series

*The Depth of Darkness*

*Into The Darkness*

*Deliver Us From Darkness*

## Cassie Quinn Series

*Path of Bones*

*Whisper of Bones*

*Symphony of Bones*

*Etched in Shadow*

*Concealed in Shadow (2022)*

## Blake Brier Series

*Unmasked*

*Unleashed*

*Uncharted*

*Drawpoint*

*Contrail*

*Detachment*

*Clear (Coming Soon)*

## Dalton Savage Series

*Savage Grounds*

*Scorched Earth*

*Cold Sky (Coming Soon)*

## Maddie Castle Series

*The Handler*

*Tracking Justice (Coming Soon)*

## Affliction Z Series

*Affliction Z: Patient Zero*

*Affliction Z: Abandoned Hope*

*Affliction Z: Descended in Blood*

*Affliction Z : Fractured Part 1*

*Affliction Z: Fractured Part 2 (Fall 2021)*

# ABOUT THE AUTHOR

L.T. Ryan is a *USA Today* and international bestselling author. The new age of publishing offered L.T. the opportunity to blend his passions for creating, marketing, and technology to reach audiences with his popular Jack Noble series.

Living in central Virginia with his wife, the youngest of his three daughters, and their three dogs, L.T. enjoys staring out his window at the trees and mountains while he should be writing, as well as reading, hiking, running, and playing with gadgets. See what he's up to at http://ltryan.com.

**Social Medial Links:**

- Facebook (L.T. Ryan): https://www.facebook.com/LTRyanAuthor

- Facebook (Jack Noble Page): https://www.facebook.com/JackNobleBooks/

- Twitter: https://twitter.com/LTRyanWrites

- Goodreads: http://www.goodreads.com/author/show/6151659.L_T_Ryan